William James Rolfe, Walter Scott

Tales of Chivalry and the Olden Time

William James Rolfe, Walter Scott

Tales of Chivalry and the Olden Time

ISBN/EAN: 9783744742665

Printed in Europe, USA, Canada, Australia, Japan

Cover: Foto ©Andreas Hilbeck / pixelio.de

More available books at **www.hansebooks.com**

SIR WALTER SCOTT.

English Classics for School Reading.

TALES OF CHIVALRY

AND THE OLDEN TIME,

SELECTED FROM THE WORKS

OF

SIR WALTER SCOTT.

EDITED, WITH NOTES,

BY

WILLIAM J. ROLFE, LITT. D.

ILLUSTRATED.

NEW YORK:
HARPER & BROTHERS, FRANKLIN SQUARE.
1895.

PREFACE.

THE series of which this is the initial volume was planned more than six years ago, and three years have passed since the plan was approved by the publishers; but its execution has been delayed by work upon other books. My aim is to edit certain selections from standard prose and poetry suited either for "supplementary reading," as it is called, or for elementary *study* in English literature. The brief foot-notes under the text are perhaps all that some teachers will regard as necessary for the former purpose; but I believe that the longer notes at the end of the book will be found more or less useful and suggestive for oral instruction in connection with the reading-lessons. These latter notes, however, are more especially designed for the other purpose I have mentioned—elementary *study* of language and literature. They have been prepared with much care, and I am confident that they will be perfectly intelligible to boys and girls in grammar schools and others of similar grade. I shall not attempt here to explain how I think they should be used, as the little pamphlet of "Hints to Teachers," which may be obtained, post-free, on application to the publishers, will give my views more in detail than would be possible in a preface. Suffice it to say now, to forestall possible criticism, that these notes are *not* designed to give *systematic* instruction in either grammar or rhetoric.

The sketches of the life of Scott are my own. For the condensed extracts from his works I have been largely indebted to a little book (without notes) published in England forty years ago, and long since out of print. "The Crusaders" is from the *Tales of a Grandfather;* "The Christian Knight and the Saracen," from *The Talisman;* and all the rest from *Ivanhoe.*

W. J. R.

CAMBRIDGE, *July* 19, 1887.

SCOTT'S CHAIR, ABBOTSFORD.

CONTENTS.

OLD HIGH SCHOOL, EDINBURGH.

ILLUSTRATIONS.

ABBOTSFORD.

THE EARLY LIFE OF SCOTT.

WALTER SCOTT was born in Edinburgh on the 15th of August, 1771. His father was a successful lawyer, and his mother was the daughter of Dr. John Rutherford, professor of medicine in the University of Edinburgh. In an account of his own life which Scott began, he says:

"I showed every sign of health and strength until I was about eighteen months old. One night, I have been often told, I showed great reluctance to be caught and put to bed, and, after being chased about the room, was apprehended and consigned to my dormitory with some difficulty. It was the last time I was to show such personal agility. In the morning I was discovered to be affected with the fever which often accompanies the cutting of large teeth. It held me three days. On the fourth, when they went to bathe me as usual, they discovered that I had lost the power of my right leg. . . . There appeared to be no dislocation or sprain; blisters and other topical remedies were applied in vain."

By the advice of Dr. Rutherford, the child was sent to reside with his paternal grandfather in the country, in order to "give the chance of natural exertion, excited

I

by free air and liberty ;" and here, at the farmhouse of
Sandy-Knowe, as it was called, he spent the next two
years.   25

The epistle prefixed to the 3d Canto of *Marmion* con-
tains a charming picture of the infant poet's feelings
amid the scenery and associations of Sandy - Knowe.
He says :

> Thus while I ape the measure wild   30
> Of tales that charmed me yet a child,
> Rude though they be, still with the chime
> Return the thoughts of early time ;
> And feelings, roused in life's first day,
> Glow in the line and prompt the lay.   35
> Then rise those crags, that mountain tower [1]
> Which charmed my fancy's wakening hour,
> Though no broad river swept along,
> To claim perchance heroic song,
> Though sighed no groves in summer gale,   40
> To prompt of love a softer tale,
> Though scarce a puny streamlet's speed
> Claimed homage from a shepherd's reed, [2]
> Yet was poetic impulse given
> By the green hill and clear blue heaven.   45
> It was a barren scene and wild,
> Where naked cliffs were rudely piled,
> But ever and anon between
> Lay velvet tufts of loveliest green ;

---

[1] This was Smailholm Tower, the ruined remnant of an old baro-
nial castle near Sandy-Knowe. Scott afterwards made it the scene
of his ballad, *The Eve of Saint John.* It is about two miles from
Dryburgh Abbey, where the poet is buried.

[2] That is, was celebrated in pastoral poetry. The *reed*, or pipe
on which the shepherd plays, is often used as the symbol of such
poetry.

And well the lonely infant knew 50
Recesses where the wall-flower grew,
And honeysuckle loved to crawl
Up the low crag and ruined wall.
I deemed such nooks the sweetest shade
The sun in all its round surveyed, 55
And still I thought that shattered tower
The mightiest work of human power,
And marvelled as the aged hind [1]
With some strange tale bewitched my mind
Of forayers, who with headlong force 60
Down from that strength [2] had spurred their horse,
Their southern rapine to renew
Far in the distant Cheviots blue,
And, home returning, filled the hall
With revel, wassail-rout, and brawl. 65
Methought that still with trump and clang
The gateway's broken arches rang;
Methought grim features, seamed with scars,
Glared through the window's rusty bars,
And ever, by the winter hearth, 70
Old tales I heard of woe or mirth,
Of lovers' sleights, [3] of ladies' charms,
Of witches' spells, of warriors' arms;
Of patriot battles, won of old
By Wallace wight [4] and Bruce the bold; 75
Of later fields of feud and fight,
When, pouring from their Highland height,

[1] The "aged hind" was "Auld Sandy Ormiston," the cow-herd of the farm, and the favorite companion of Walter. Lockhart says: "If the child saw him in the morning, he could not be satisfied unless the old man would set him astride on his shoulder, and take him to keep him company as he lay watching his charge."

[2] Stronghold; the abstract noun used for the concrete.

[3] Stratagems. The word is misprinted "slights" in almost all the editions of Scott.   [4] Gallant, warlike.

The Scottish clans in headlong sway
Had swept the scarlet ranks[1] away.
While stretched at length upon the floor,   80
Again I fought each combat o'er,
Pebbles and shells, in order laid,
The mimic ranks of war displayed;
And onward still the Scottish Lion bore,
And still the scattered Southron fled before.   85
   Still, with vain fondness, could I trace
Anew each kind familiar face
That brightened at our evening fire!
From the thatched mansion's grey-haired sire,[2]
Wise without learning, plain and good,   90
And sprung of Scotland's gentler blood;
Whose eye in age, quick, clear, and keen,
Showed what in youth its glance had been;
Whose doom discording neighbours sought,
Content with equity unbought;   95
To him the venerable priest,[3]
Our frequent and familiar guest,
Whose life and manners well could paint
Alike the student and the saint,
Alas! whose speech too oft I broke   100
With gambol rude and timeless[4] joke:
For I was wayward, bold, and wild,
A self-willed imp, a grandame's child,
But half a plague, and half a jest,
Was still endured, beloved, caressed.   105

When spending a summer day in his old age amid
these well-remembered scenes, Scott told a friend that

---

[1] The English soldiers, or "red-coats."

[2] Robert Scott, the child's grandfather.

[3] Rev. John Martin, clergyman of the parish in which Sandy-
Knowe is situated. See the next page.

[4] Made at the wrong time, inopportune.

he used to delight in rolling about on the grass all day long in the midst of the flock, and that "the sort of fellowship he thus formed with the sheep and lambs had impressed his mind with a degree of affectionate feeling towards them which had lasted throughout life." There is a story of his having been forgotten one day among the knolls when a thunder-storm came on ; and his aunt, suddenly recollecting his situation, and running out to bring him home, is said to have found him lying on his back, clapping his hands at the lightning, and crying out " Bonny ! bonny !" at every flash.

Scott's grandmother used to tell him many a tale of Wat of Harden and the other Border heroes of the olden time ; and his aunt Janet would read to him from Ramsay's *Tea-table Miscellany* and other books, until he could repeat long passages by heart. He says :

" The ballad of *Hardyknute* I was early master of, to the great annoyance of almost our only visitor, the worthy clergyman of the parish, who had not patience to have a sober chat interrupted by my shouting forth this ditty. Methinks I now see his tall, thin, emaciated figure, his legs cased in clasped gambadoes,[1] and his face of a length that would have rivalled the Knight of La Mancha's,[2] and hear him exclaim, 'One may as well speak in the mouth of a cannon as where that child is.'"

When Walter was four years old he was taken to Bath in England, where it was thought the waters might help his lameness. His health was now a good deal confirmed by country air and exercise, and he had become able by degrees to stand, to walk, and to run. " I, who

---

[1] A kind of gaiters worn to protect the legs from mud when walking or riding.

[2] Don Quixote, the hero of the famous Spanish novel.

in a city," he says, " had probably been condemned to
hopeless and helpless decrepitude, was now a healthy,
high-spirited, and, my lameness apart, a sturdy child." 140

He spent a year at Bath, with little or no advantage
to his lameness ; but during this time he " acquired the
rudiments of reading at a day school kept by an old
dame." He adds :

" But the most delightful recollections of Bath are 145
dated after the arrival of my uncle, Captain Robert Scott,
who introduced me to all the little amusements which
suited my age, and above all to the theatre. The play
was *As You Like It;* and the witchery of the whole
scene is alive in my mind at this moment. I made, I 150
believe, noise more than enough, and remember being
so much scandalized at the quarrel between Orlando
and his brother, in the first scene, that I screamed out,
' A'n't they brothers?' A few weeks' residence at home
convinced me, who had till then been an only child in 155
the house of my grandfather, that a quarrel between
brothers was a very natural event."

After the year at Bath, Walter returned first to Edinburgh and afterwards for a season to Sandy-Knowe.
When he was a year or two older it was thought that 160
sea-bathing might be of service to his lameness, and his
aunt took him to Prestonpans. There he made the acquaintance of an old soldier named Dalgetty, to whom
he refers as follows :

" As this old gentleman, who had been in all the Ger- 165
man wars, found very few to listen to his tales of military feats, he formed a sort of alliance with me, and I
used invariably to attend him for the pleasure of hearing these communications. Sometimes our conversation
turned on the American war, which was then raging. It 170

was about the time of Burgoyne's unfortunate expedition, to which my captain and I augured different conclusions. Somebody had showed me a map of North America, and, struck with the rugged appearance of the country and the quantity of lakes, I expressed some 175 doubts on the subject of the general's arriving safely at the end of his journey, which were very indignantly refuted by the captain. The news of the Saratoga disaster,[1] while it gave me a little triumph, rather shook my intimacy with the veteran." 180

At Prestonpans the young Scott met also with George Constable, who was the original of Jonathan Oldbuck in the novel of *The Antiquary*. He told the child "about Falstaff and Hotspur and other characters in Shakespeare," and Scott says that he remembers being inter- 185 ested in the subject, which would seem to be beyond his comprehension at that early age. He adds: "In-

---

[1] Scott speaks of this intimacy with Captain Dalgetty as being when he was in his eighth year; but as the surrender at Saratoga was in October, 1777, he was little more than six years old at the time.

A letter written by Mrs. Cockburn presents an interesting picture of Scott at six: "I last night supped in Mr. Walter Scott's. He has the most extraordinary genius of a boy I ever saw. He was reading a poem to his mother when I went in. I made him read on; it was the description of a shipwreck. His passion rose with the storm. He lifted his eyes and hands. 'There's the mast gone,' says he; 'crash it goes!—they will all perish!' After his agitation, he turns to me: 'That is too melancholy; I had better read you something more amusing.' I preferred a little chat, and asked his opinion of Milton and other books he was reading, which he gave me wonderfully. . . . When taken to bed last night, he told his aunt he liked that lady [the writer], 'for I think she is a virtuoso like myself.'—'Dear Walter,' says Aunt Jenny, 'what is a virtuoso?'— 'Don't ye know? Why, it's one who wishes and will know everything.'"

deed, I rather suspect that children derive impulses of
a powerful and important kind in hearing things which
they cannot entirely comprehend, and therefore that to 190
write *down* to children's understanding is a mistake:
set them on the scent, and let them puzzle it out."

After the stay at Prestonpans Walter returned to Edinburgh, where he continued to reside for the most part
until his marriage. His mother had "a strong turn to 195
study poetry and works of imagination," and his leisure
hours were usually spent in reading aloud to her from
Pope's translation of Homer, which, excepting a few
ballads and songs, was the first poetry he had perused.
He says in this connection :   200

"My mother had good natural taste and great feeling : she used to make me pause upon those passages
which expressed generous and worthy sentiments, and
if she could not divert me from those which were de-
scriptive of battle and tumult, she contrived at least to 205
divide my attention between them. My own enthusiasm,
however, was chiefly awakened by the wonderful and
the terrible—the common taste of children, but in which
I have remained a child even unto this day. I got by
heart, not as a task but almost without intending it, the 210
passages with which I was most pleased, and used to
recite them aloud, both when alone and to others—more
willingly, however, in my hours of solitude, for I had
observed some auditors smile, and I dreaded ridicule
at that time of life more than I have ever done since." 215

In 1778 Walter was sent to the High School of Edinburgh, then taught by Mr. Luke Fraser. Though he
had studied Latin under a private teacher, he was somewhat behind the class in which he was now placed, and
this disadvantage he appears never to have overcome. 220

"I did not make any great figure at the High School,"
he tells us; "or, at least, any exertions which I made
were desultory and little to be depended on." His rela-
tions with his schoolmates were on the whole more
pleasant than with his teachers. He says:

"Among my companions my good-nature and a flow
of ready imagination rendered me very popular. Boys
are uncommonly just in their feelings, and at least
equally generous. My lameness, and the efforts which
I made to supply that disadvantage, by making up in
address what I wanted in activity, engaged the latter
principle in my favor; and in the winter play - hours,
when hard exercise was impossible, my tales used to
assemble an admiring audience round Lucky Brown's
fireside, and happy was he that could sit next to the
inexhaustible narrator. I was also, though often negligent of my own task, always ready to assist my friends;
and hence I had a little party of stanch partisans and
adherents, stout of hand and heart, though somewhat
dull of head—the very tools for raising a hero to eminence. So, on the whole, I made a brighter figure in
the *yards* than in the *class*. . . .

"After having been three years under Mr. Fraser, our
class was, in the usual routine of the school, turned over
to Dr. Adam, the Rector. It was from this respectable
man that I first learned the value of the knowledge I
had hitherto considered only as a burdensome task. It
was the fashion to remain two years at his class, where
we read Cæsar and Livy and Sallust, in prose; Virgil,
Horace, and Terence, in verse. I had by this time
mastered, in some degree, the difficulties of the language,
and began to be sensible of its beauties. This was really
gathering grapes from thistles; nor shall I soon forget

the swelling of my little pride when the Rector pronounced, that, though many of my school-fellows understood the Latin better, *Gualterus Scott* was behind few 255
in following and enjoying the author's meaning. Thus
encouraged, I distinguished myself by some attempts at
poetical versions from Horace and Virgil.' Dr. Adam
used to invite his scholars to such essays, but never
made them tasks. I gained some distinction upon these 260
occasions, and the Rector in future took much notice
of me ; and his judicious mixture of censure and praise
went far to counterbalance my habits of indolence and
inattention. I saw I was expected to do well, and I was
piqued in honor to vindicate my master's favorable 265
opinion. I climbed, therefore, to the first form ; and,
though I never made a first-rate Latinist, my school-fellows, and, what was of more consequence, I myself, considered that I had a character for learning to maintain. . . .   270

' Lockhart informs us that "one of these little pieces, written in
a weak boyish scrawl, within pencil marks still visible, had been
carefully preserved by his mother." It was folded up in a cover
inscribed by the old lady, "My Walter's first lines, 1782" (when he
was eleven years old), and reads thus :

> " In awful ruins Ætna thunders nigh,
>   And sends in pitchy whirlwinds to the sky
>   Black clouds of smoke, which, still as they aspire,
>   From their dark sides there bursts the glowing fire;
>   At other times huge balls of fire are toss'd,
>   That lick the stars and in the smoke are lost:
>   Sometimes the mount, with vast convulsions torn,
>   Emits huge rocks, which instantly are borne
>   With loud explosions to the starry skies,
>   The stones made liquid as the huge mass flies,
>   Then back again with greater weight recoils,
>   While Ætna thundering from the bottom boils."

This is evidently a version of Virgil's *Æneid*, iii. 571-577.

"From Dr. Adam's class I should, according to the usual routine, have proceeded immediately to college. But, fortunately, I was not yet to lose, by a total dismission from constraint, the acquaintance with the Latin which I had acquired. My health had become rather 275 delicate from rapid growth, and my father was easily persuaded to allow me to spend half a year at Kelso with my kind aunt, Miss Janet Scott. . . . My time was here left entirely to my own disposal, excepting for about four hours in the day, when I was expected to at- 280 tend the grammar-school[1] of the village. The teacher at that time was Mr. Lancelot Whale, an excellent classical scholar, a humorist, and a worthy man. . . . I made considerable progress under his instructions. . . . I acted as usher, and heard the inferior classes, and I 285 spouted the speech of Galgacus at the public examination, which did not make the less impression on the audience that few of them probably understood one word of it.

"In the meanwhile my acquaintance with English lit- 290 erature was gradually extending itself. In the intervals of my school hours I had always perused with avidity such books of history or poetry or voyages and travels as chance presented to me,—not forgetting the usual, or rather ten times the usual, quantity of fairy tales, Eastern 295 stories, romances, etc. These studies were totally unregulated and undirected. My tutor thought it almost a sin to open a profane play or poem ; and my mother, besides that she might be in some degree trammelled by the religious scruples which he suggested, had no 300 longer the opportunity to hear me read poetry as for-

---

[1] Not a grammar-school in the American sense, but a Latin school.

merly. I found, however, in her dressing-room (where I slept at one time) some odd volumes of Shakespeare; nor can I easily forget the rapture with which I sate up in my shirt reading them by the light of a fire in her apartment, until the bustle of the family rising from supper warned me it was time to creep back to my bed, where I was supposed to have been safely deposited since nine o'clock. Chance, however, threw in my way a poetical preceptor. This was no other than the excellent and benevolent Dr. Blacklock, well known at that time as a literary character. . . . The kind old man opened to me the stores of his library, and through his recommendation I became intimate with Ossian and Spenser. I was delighted with both, yet I think chiefly with the latter poet. The tawdry repetitions of the Ossianic phraseology disgusted me rather sooner than might have been expected from my age. But Spenser I could have read forever. Too young to trouble myself about the allegory, I considered all the knights and ladies and dragons and giants in their outward and exoteric [1] sense, and God only knows how delighted I was to find myself in such society. As I had always a wonderful facility in retaining in my memory whatever verses pleased me, the quantity of Spenser's stanzas which I could repeat was really marvellous. But this memory of mine was a very fickle ally, and has through my whole life acted merely upon its own capricious motion. . . . It seldom failed to preserve most tenaciously a favorite passage of poetry, a playhouse ditty, or, above all, a Border-raid ballad; but names, dates, and the other technicalities of history escaped me in a most melancholy degree. The philosophy of history,

[1] Obvious.

a much more important subject, was also a sealed book at this period of my life; but I gradually assembled 335 much of what was striking and picturesque in historical narrative; and when, in riper years, I attended more to the deduction of general principles, I was furnished with a powerful host of examples in illustration of them. . . .

"I left the High School, therefore, with a great quan- 340 tity of general information, ill arranged, indeed, and collected without system, yet deeply impressed upon my mind; readily assorted by my power of connection and memory, and gilded, if I may be permitted to say so, by a vivid and active imagination. If my studies were not 345 under any direction at Edinburgh, in the country, it may be well imagined, they were less so. A respectable subscription library, a circulating library of ancient standing, and some private book-shelves were open to my random perusal, and I waded into the stream like a 350 blind man into a ford, without the power of searching my way, unless by groping for it. My appetite for books was as ample and indiscriminating as it was indefatigable, and I since have had too frequently reason to repent that few ever read so much, and to so little purpose. . . . 355

"I then first became acquainted with Bishop Percy's *Reliques of Ancient Poetry.* . . . I remember well the spot where I read these volumes for the first time. It was beneath a huge platanus-tree,[1] in the ruins of what had been intended for an old-fashioned arbor in the 360 garden I have mentioned. The summer-day sped onward so fast, that, notwithstanding the sharp appetite of thirteen, I forgot the hour of dinner, was sought for with anxiety, and was still found entranced in my intellect-

---

[1] Plane-tree. In Scotland the name is commonly given to the sycamore.

ual banquet.   To read and to remember was in this 365
instance the same thing, and henceforth I overwhelmed
my school-fellows, and all who would hearken to me,
with tragical recitations from the ballads of Bishop Percy.   The first time, too, I could scrape a few shillings
together, which were not common occurrences with me, 370
I bought unto myself a copy of these beloved volumes;
nor do I believe I ever read a book half so frequently,
or with half the enthusiasm.   About this period also I
became acquainted with the works of Richardson, and
those of Mackenzie (whom in later years I became en- 375
titled to call my friend), with Fielding, Smollett, and
some others of our best novelists.

   "To this period also I can trace distinctly the awak-
ing of that delightful feeling for the beauties of natural
objects which has never since deserted me.   The neigh- 380
borhood of Kelso, the most beautiful if not the most
romantic village in Scotland, is eminently calculated to
awaken these ideas.   It presents objects, not only grand
in themselves, but venerable from their associations. . . .
The romantic feelings which I have described as pre- 385
dominating in my mind, naturally rested upon and associated themselves with these grand features of the
landscape around me; and the historical incidents or
traditional legends connected with many of them gave
to my admiration a sort of intense impression of rever- 390
ence, which at times made my heart feel too big for its
bosom.   From this time the love of natural beauty,
more especially when combined with ancient ruins, or
remains of our fathers' piety or splendor, became with
me an insatiable passion, which, if circumstances had 395
permitted, I would willingly have gratified by travelling
over half the globe."

Scott returned to Edinburgh and resumed his studies in the College, where he began Greek under the same disadvantage with which he had started in Latin, his ₄₀₀ companions having already learned the elements of the language. One of them, who was an excellent scholar, told Walter that he was "distinguished by the name of the *Greek blockhead,*" and exhorted him to redeem his reputation, but to no purpose. Later his teacher de- ₄₀₅ clared that "dunce he was, and dunce was to remain." In after-life he says he "forgot the very letters of the Greek alphabet."

Of mathematics he got "a very superficial smatter-ing," but made some progress in ethics under Professor ₄₁₀ John Bruce, and "was selected as one of his students whose progress he approved, to read an essay before Principal Robertson." He also studied moral philosophy (under Dugald Stewart) and history, but little else until he began his legal studies. "So that," he says, "if my ₄₁₅ learning be flimsy and inaccurate, the reader must have some compassion even for an idle workman who had so narrow a foundation to build upon. If, however, it should ever fall to the lot of youth to peruse these pages —let such a reader remember, that it is with the deepest ₄₂₀ regret that I recollect in my manhood the opportunities of learning which I neglected in my youth; that through every part of my literary career I have felt pinched and hampered by my own ignorance; and that I would at this moment give half the reputation I have had the ₄₂₅ good-fortune to acquire, if by doing so I could rest the remaining part upon a sound foundation of learning and science."

THE LATER LIFE OF SCOTT.

To the somewhat detailed account of Scott's early years given in the preceding pages, we may add a brief sketch of his after-life.

In 1792 he was admitted to the Scottish bar. Through his father's influence he obtained some employment, but 5 not enough to keep him busy. It was not, however, until 1796 that he turned his attention to literature. In that year he published translations of the German Bürger's ballads, *Lenore* and *The Wild Huntsman*. These attracted some attention, and led to his contributing a 10 few pieces to Lewis's *Tales of Wonder*. In 1799 he translated Goethe's *Götz von Berlichingen*. In 1802 he published the first two volumes of the *Border Minstrelsy*, printed by his old schoolmate Ballantyne, who had just set up in business at Kelso. The work was received 15 with great favor, which was augmented by the appearance of the third volume (1803) containing some original imitations of the old ballads.

The next important event in Scott's literary life was the publication of *The Lay of the Last Minstrel* in 1805. 20 Its success was extraordinary, and the author became at once the most popular poet of the day. *Marmion* followed in 1808, and *The Lady of the Lake* in 1810. With the latter his poetic fame may be said to have reached its height. *The Vision of Don Roderick, Rokeby, The Lord* 25 *of the Isles*, and other poems that followed, were not so well received.

Meanwhile Scott had been appointed Sheriff of Selkirkshire and one of the clerks of the Court of Session, the combined salaries being about £1800 ($9000) a 30 year, independent of his large receipts from his books. He became ambitious to be a large landed proprietor, and ran into debt by the purchase of the estate of Abbotsford and the erection of the mansion, to which he removed in 1812. He also engaged in unfortunate com- 35 mercial transactions to which reference will be made farther on.

The decline in his popularity as a poet had turned his thoughts to the almost forgotten manuscript of *Waverley*, which he had begun nine years before, but had laid aside 40 on account of the discouraging comments of a friend to whom he had shown it. He now resolved to complete it, and it was published anonymously in 1814. The unknown "author of Waverley" leaped into greater fame than the poet Scott had attained by the *Lay* and *Mar-* 45 *mion;* but he preserved his incognito, and sent forth *Guy Mannering, The Antiquary, Rob Roy*, etc., in rapid succession and with ever-increasing renown. Carlyle, who lived through all the excitement, says: "Hardly any literary reputation ever rose so high in our island; 50 no reputation at all ever spread so wide. Walter Scott became Sir Walter Scott, Baronet, of Abbotsford, on whom fortune seemed to pour her whole cornucopia of wealth, honor, and worldly good, the favorite of princes and of peasants and all intermediate men. His *Waverley* 55

2

series, swift following one on the other apparently without
end, was the universal reading; looked for like an an-
nual harvest, by all ranks, in all European countries."

Scott himself was naturally led to regard his literary
powers as an exhaustless mine of wealth, and became 60
more and more extravagant in enlarging his estate, fitting up Abbotsford, and exercising a generous hospitality. Unknown to his friends he had also become a
partner in the printing business of the Ballantynes; and
when the house failed, owing to the bankruptcy of the 65
publisher Constable in 1826, he found himself a debtor
to the extent of £120,000 ($600,000).

The catastrophe would have crushed most men, but
Scott determined to pay off the heavy debt with his pen
if his creditors would allow him time. He disclosed the 70
secret of the Waverley authorship, and began a new novel
at once. This was *Woodstock*, which brought his creditors £8000 ($40,000). His *Life of Napoleon*, written with
almost incredible speed and published the next year
(1827), realized from the first and second editions £18- 75
000 more. In two years Scott paid off £40,000 of his
debts, and in the course of four years almost £70,000.
But the strain upon his powers of mind and body was
too severe, and in 1831 he was led to give up literary work
for a time and make a tour to the Continent. He spent 80
five months in Italy, in the hope of regaining his health;
but it was too late. "There are glimpses in the me-
moirs of that time—glimpses inexpressibly sad—of the
dying man in Italy, at Naples, on the Campagna.[1] It
is only the shadow of the stalwart Scott. He sits for 85
hours gazing upon the sea; he moves restlessly about;

---

[1] The Roman Campagna (Italian for open country), the desolate
plain surrounding the city of Rome.

he repeats, in a tone so mournful that the heart breaks to hear, snatches of the old, old ballads that his youth loved, and which are dear to all men who speak his language because he loved them.   Then he comes home to die.   Gentle as a child, he has been unspoiled by the flattery of a world.   Through the mists of the fast-fading mind looks out that true and tender manhood which is forever memorable.   'Be a good man, my dear,' he whispers to his son-in-law Lockhart, and on a soft September afternoon, with all the windows wide open, and the gentle ripple of the Tweed murmuring upon the air, while his children knelt around the bed, Walter Scott died, 'and his eldest son kissed and closed his eyes.'"

It was in June, 1832, that Scott returned to England, and his death occurred on the 21st of September following.   He was buried in St. Mary's Aisle, the most beautiful part of the ruined Dryburgh Abbey, in the tomb of his ancestors, the Haliburtons of Newmains, who were at one time proprietors of the abbey.   His wife, who died six years before him, lies by his side. His eldest son, Sir Walter Scott, and his son-in-law and biographer Lockhart are also buried here.

Scott's children were all dead within fifteen years of his own decease, and at the present time (1887) only one of his direct descendants survives—Mary Monica Hope-Scott, the grandchild of Mrs. Lockhart and great-grandchild of the founder of Abbotsford.

DRYBURGH ABBEY.

TALES OF CHIVALRY AND THE OLDEN TIME.

THE CRUSADERS.

THE devotional journeys, called pilgrimages, to the tombs of the religious persons mentioned in Scripture, or the places where they had wrought their miracles, were accounted meritorious displays of piety, the performance of which, by the tenets of the Catholic Church, was held the surest and most acceptable mode of averting the wrath of Heaven for past transgressions, or exhibiting gratitude for mercies received. Men who were in difficulties or in dangers often made a vow, that, in the event of their being extricated, they would make a journey to some sanctified shrine in Italy or in Palestine, and there testify their sense of the protection of Heaven, by alms, prayers, and gifts to the church. The Holy Sepulchre itself, of which the site was handed down by tradition, was naturally a principal object of these religious peregrinations, as best entitled to the respect and adoration of all Christians.

While Palestine remained a part of the Grecian or Eastern Empire, the access of the European pilgrims to the holy places which they desired to visit, was naturally facilitated by every means in the power of the Christian governors of the provinces where they lay, and of the priests to whose keeping these places were committed. Their churches were enriched by the gifts which failed not to express the devotion of the pilgrims, and 25 the vanity of the priests was flattered by the resort of so many persons of consequence from the most distant parts of Christendom, to worship at their peculiar shrines.

Even when, in the course of the tenth century, the Holy Land fell under the power of the Saracens, that 30 people, although votaries of another faith, felt their own interest in permitting, under payment of a certain capitation tax,[1] the concourse of European pilgrims to Jerusalem, and other places which they accounted sacred. But when the power of the Saracens was in a great meas- 35 ure divided or destroyed, and the Turks, also followers of Mahomet, but a far more rude and fanatical race, became masters of Jerusalem, the treatment of the Christians, whether natives of Palestine or pilgrims who came to worship there, was in every respect changed for the 40 worse. The Saracens, a civilized and refined people compared with the Turks, had governed the country under fixed rules of tribute, and preferred the moderate but secure profit derived from the taxes imposed on the pilgrims, to that which might be obtained by a system 45 of robbery, plunder, and ill-usage. But the Turks, a fiercer, more bigoted, and more short-sighted race, preferred the pleasure of insulting and maltreating the Christians, whom they contemned and hated, and not only harassed them by the most exorbitant exactions, but often 50 added to these personal ill-usage of the most revolting kind. The pilgrims were entirely at the mercy of every paltry Turkish officer, and an act of devotion, in itself perilous and expensive, was rendered too frequently an

---

[1] Poll-tax, or a tax on each person.

RICHARD I. OF ENGLAND.

introduction to martyrdom. The clergy of the Chris-55
tians were insulted, stripped, and thrown into dungeons ;
nor was any circumstance omitted by the savage masters of the Holy City which could show the pilgrims at
how great a hazard they must in future expect permission to pay their homage there.   60

These evils had been sufficiently felt by all who had
visited the East, but at length they made so strong an
impression on the spirit of one man that, like fire alighting among materials highly combustible, the flame spread
throughout all Europe. The person who effected so great 65
a sensation by such slight means was called Peter the
Hermit. He was, we are informed, of a slight and indifferent figure, which sometimes exposed him to be neglected ; but he was a powerful orator. He had himself
been a pilgrim in Palestine, and possessed the impres- 70
sive requisite that he could bear testimony as an eye-wit-
ness to the atrocities of the Turks and the sufferings of
the Christians. He repaired from court to court, from
castle to castle, from city to city, setting forth at each
the shame done to Christendom, in leaving the holiest 75
places connected with her religion in possession of a
heathen and barbarous foe. He appealed to the religion of one sovereign, to the fears of another, to the spirit
of chivalry professed by them all. Urban II., then Pope,
saw the importance of uniting the European nations, sol- 80
diers by habit and inclination, in a task so honorable to
religion, and so likely to give importance to the Roman
See. At the Council of Clermont [A.D. 1095], ambas-
sadors from the Grecian emperor were introduced to the
assembly, who, with humble deference, stated to the 85
prelates and the lay chivalry of Europe the dangers to
their Christian sovereign, arising from the increasing

strength of the Moslem empire, by which he was surrounded, and, forgetting the wordy and assuming language which they were accustomed to use, supplicated, 90
with humiliating earnestness, the advantage of some as-
sistance from Europe. The Pontiff himself set forth the
advantage, or rather necessity, of laying all meaner or
more worldly tasks aside, until the Holy Land should
be freed from the heathen usurpers who were its tyrants. 95
To all, however criminal, who should lend aid to this
sacred warfare, Urban promised a full remission of their
sins here, and an indubitable portion of the joys of heaven
hereafter. He then appealed to the temporal princes,
with the enthusiastic quotation of such texts of Script- 100
ure as were most likely to inflame their natural valor.
"Gird on your swords," he said, "ye men of valor; it
is our part to pray, it is yours to fight. It is ours, with
Moses,[1] to hold up our hands unremittingly to God; it
is yours to stretch out the sword against the children of 105
Amalek.—So be it." The assembly answered, as to a
summons blown by an archangel, "It is the will of
God—it is the will of God!" Thousands devoted themselves to the service of God, as they imagined, and to
the recovery of Palestine, with its shrines, from the hands 110
of the Turks, and, as a mark of being enlisted in the
service, began to wear the figure of a cross on the shoulder of their cloak, but of a different color from that of
the garment itself. From this cross the undertaking
was called a *Crusade,* and those who were engaged in 115
it *Crusaders.* The eagerness with which this holy symbol was adopted was so great that some of the princes
cut their robes in pieces, in order to furnish crosses for
the multitudes around.

---

[1] See *Exodus,* xvii. 8-13.

THE CHRISTIAN KNIGHT AND THE SARACEN.

THE burning sun of Syria had not yet attained its highest point in the heavens, when a knight of the Red-cross, who had left his distant northern home and joined the host of the Crusaders in Palestine, was pacing slowly along the sandy deserts which lie in the vicinity of the 5 Dead Sea, or, as it is called, the Lake Asphaltites, where the waves of the Jordan pour themselves into an inland sea, from which there is no discharge of waters.

The warlike pilgrim had toiled among cliffs and precipices during the earlier part of the morning ; more lately, 10 issuing from those rocky and dangerous defiles, he had entered upon that great plain[1] where the accursed cities provoked in ancient days the direct and dreadful vengeance of the Omnipotent.

The toil, the thirst, the dangers of the way were for- 15 gotten, as the traveller recalled the fearful catastrophe which had converted into an arid and dismal wilderness the fair and fertile valley of Siddim, once well watered, even as the Garden of the Lord, now a parched and blighted waste, condemned to eternal sterility. 20

Crossing himself, as he viewed the dark mass of roll-

[1] The Plain of Jordan, in which Sodom and Gomorrah were situated. See *Genesis*, xiii. 10-13, etc.

ing waters, in color as in quality unlike those of every other lake, the traveller shuddered as he remembered that beneath these sluggish waves lay the once proud cities of the plain, whose grave was dug by the thunder [25] of the heavens, or the eruption of subterraneous fire, and whose remains were hid, even by that sea which holds no living fish in its bosom, bears no skiff on its surface, and, as if its own dreadful bed were the only fit receptacle for its sullen waters, sends not, like other lakes, a [30] tribute to the ocean. The whole land around, as in the days of Moses, was " brimstone and salt ; it is not sown, nor beareth, nor any grass groweth thereon ;" [1] the land as well as the lake might be termed dead, as producing nothing having resemblance to vegetation, and even the [35] very air was entirely devoid of its ordinary winged inhabitants, deterred probably by the odor of bitumen and sulphur, which the burning sun exhaled from the waters of the lake in steaming clouds, frequently assuming the appearance of waterspouts. Masses of the slimy and [40] sulphurous substance called naphtha, which floated idly on the sluggish and sullen waves, supplied those rolling clouds with new vapors, and afforded awful testimony to the truth of the Mosaic history.

Upon this scene of desolation the sun shone with al- [45] most intolerable splendor, and all living nature seemed to have hidden itself from the rays, excepting the solitary figure which appeared the sole breathing thing on the wide surface of the plain. The dress of the rider and the accoutrements of his horse were peculiarly unfit [50] for the traveller in such a country. A coat of linked mail, with long sleeves, plated gauntlets, and a steel breast-plate, had not been esteemed a sufficient weight

---

[1] See *Deuteronomy*, xxix. 23.

of armor; there was also his triangular shield suspended round his neck, and his barred helmet of steel, 55
over which he had a hood and collar of mail, which was
drawn around the warrior's shoulders and throat, and
filled up the vacancy between the hauberk [1] and the
headpiece. His lower limbs were sheathed, like his
body, in flexible mail, securing the legs and thighs, while 60
the feet rested in plated shoes, which corresponded with
the gauntlets. A long, broad, straight-shaped, double-
edged falchion, with a handle formed like a cross, corresponded with a stout poniard, on the other side.
The knight also bore, secured to his saddle, with one 65
end resting on his stirrup, the long steel-headed lance,
his own proper weapon, which, as he rode, projected backwards, and displayed its little pennoncelle, [2]
to dally with the faint breeze, or drop in the dead
calm. To this cumbrous equipment must be added a 70
surcoat [3] of embroidered cloth, much frayed and worn,
which was thus far useful, that it excluded the burning
rays of the sun from the armor, which they would otherwise have rendered intolerable to the wearer. The surcoat bore, in several places, the arms [4] of the owner, al- 75
though much defaced. These seemed to be a couchant [5]
leopard, with the motto, "I sleep—wake me not." An
outline of the same device might be traced on his shield,
though many a blow had almost effaced the painting.
The flat top of his cumbrous cylindrical helmet was un- 80

[1] The coat of mail mentioned just above.

[2] Small pennon, or flag, attached to the lance. See p. 70, line 244.

[3] A loose sleeveless wrapper worn outside the armor.

[4] Figures or devices embroidered upon it, indicating who the knight
was. See *Notes*.

[5] Lying down.

adorned with any crest. In retaining their own unwieldy defensive armor, the Northern Crusaders seemed to set at defiance the nature of the climate and country to which they had come to war.

The accoutrements of the horse were scarcely less massive and unwieldy than those of the rider. The animal had a heavy saddle plated with steel, uniting in front with a species of breast-plate, and behind with defensive armor made to cover the loins. Then there was a steel axe, or hammer, called a mace-of-arms, and which hung to the saddle-bow; the reins were secured by chain-work, and the front-stall of the bridle was a steel plate, with apertures for the eyes and nostrils, having in the midst a short, sharp pike, projecting from the forehead of the horse like the horn of the fabulous unicorn.

But habit had made the endurance of this load of panoply a second nature, both to the knight and his gallant charger. Numbers, indeed, of the Western warriors who hurried to Palestine died ere they became inured to the burning climate; but there were others to whom that climate became innocent and even friendly, and among this fortunate number was the solitary horseman who now traversed the border of the Dead Sea.

Nature, which cast his limbs in a mould of uncommon strength, fitted to wear his linked hauberk with as much ease as if the meshes had been formed of cobwebs, had endowed him with a constitution as strong as his limbs, and which bade defiance to almost all changes of climate, as well as to fatigue and privations of every kind. His disposition seemed, in some degree, to partake of the qualities of his bodily frame; and as the one possessed great strength and endurance, united with the

power of violent exertion, the other, under a calm and
undisturbed semblance, had much of the fiery and en- [115]
thusiastic love of glory which constituted the principal
attribute of the renowned Norman[1] line, and had rendered them sovereigns in every corner of Europe where
they had drawn their adventurous swords.

It was not, however, to all the race that fortune pro- [120]
posed such tempting rewards; and those obtained by
the solitary knight during two years' campaign in Palestine had been only temporal fame, and, as he was taught
to believe, spiritual privileges. Meantime, his slender
stock of money had melted away, the rather that he did [125]
not pursue any of the ordinary modes by which the followers of the Crusade condescended to recruit their diminished resources, at the expense of the people of Palestine; he exacted no gifts from the wretched natives
for sparing their possessions when engaged in warfare [130]
with the Saracens, and he had not availed himself of
any opportunity of enriching himself by the ransom of
prisoners of consequence. The small train which had
followed him from his native country had been gradually diminished as the means of maintaining them dis- [135]
appeared; and his only remaining squire[2] was at present
on a sick-bed, and unable to attend his master, who trav-
elled, as we have seen, singly and alone. This was of
little consequence to the Crusader, who was accustomed
to consider his good sword as his safest escort, and de- [140]
vout thoughts as his best companion.

Nature had, however, her demands for refreshment
and repose, even on the iron frame and patient disposition of the Knight of the Sleeping Leopard; and at

[1] Belonging to *Normandy*, the northern part of France.
[2] Attendant on a knight, armor-bearer.

noon, when the Dead Sea lay at some distance on his 145
right, he joyfully hailed the sight of two or three palm-
trees, which arose beside the well which was assigned
for his midday station. His good horse, too, which
had plodded forward with the steady endurance of his
master, now lifted his head, expanded his nostrils, and 150
quickened his pace, as if he snuffed afar off the living
waters which marked the place of repose and refreshment. But labor and danger were doomed to intervene
ere the horse or horseman reached the desired spot.

As the Knight of the Couchant Leopard continued to 155
fix his eyes attentively on the yet distant cluster of palm-
trees, it seemed to him as if some object was moving
among them. The distant form separated itself from
the trees, which partly hid its motions, and advanced
towards the knight with a speed which soon showed a 160
mounted horseman, whom his turban, long spear, and
green caftan[1] floating in the wind, on his nearer approach, showed to be a Saracen cavalier. "In the desert," saith an Eastern proverb, "no man meets a friend."
The Crusader was totally indifferent whether the infidel, 165
who now approached on his gallant barb, as if borne on
the wings of an eagle, came as friend or foe—perhaps,
as a vowed champion of the Cross, he might rather have
preferred the latter. He disengaged his lance from his
saddle, seized it with the right hand, placed it in rest[2] 170
with its point half elevated, gathered up the reins in the
left, waked his horse's mettle with the spur, and prepared
to encounter the stranger with the calm self-confidence
belonging to the victor in many contests.

[1] A kind of long vest with sleeves, fastened round the waist with
a girdle; worn in Oriental countries.

[2] To lay *the spear in rest*, or *couch* it, was to put its butt in the

The Saracen came on at the speedy gallop of an 175
Arab horseman, managing his steed more by his limbs
and the inflection of his body than by any use of the
reins, which hung loose in his left hand ; so that he was
enabled to wield the light round buckler of the skin of
the rhinoceros, ornamented with silver loops, which he 180
wore on his arm, swinging it as if he meant to oppose
its slender circle to the formidable thrust of the Western
lance.   His own long spear was not couched or levelled
like that of his antagonist, but grasped by the middle
with his right hand, and brandished at arm's length above 185
his head.   As the cavalier approached his enemy at full
career, he seemed to expect that the Knight of the Leopard should put his horse to the gallop to encounter him.
But the Christian knight, well acquainted with the cus-
toms of Eastern warriors, did not mean to exhaust his 190
good horse by any unnecessary exertion ; and, on the
contrary, made a dead halt, confident that if the enemy advanced to the actual shock, his own weight, and
that of his powerful charger, would give him sufficient
advantage, without the additional momentum of rapid 195
motion.   Equally sensible and apprehensive of such a
probable result, the Saracen cavalier, when he had approached towards the Christian within twice the length
of his lance, wheeled his steed to the left with inimita-
ble dexterity, and rode twice round his antagonist, who, 200
turning without quitting his ground, and presenting his
front constantly to his enemy, frustrated his attempts to
attack him on an unguarded point ; so that the Saracen,
wheeling his horse, was fain to retreat to the distance

projection on the side of the armor called the *rest ;* that is, in posi-
tion for use in attack or defence.

of an hundred yards. A second time, like a hawk [1] at-
tacking a heron, the heathen renewed the charge, and a
second time was fain to retreat without coming to a close
struggle. A third time he approached in the same manner, when the Christian knight, desirous to terminate this
elusory warfare, in which he might at length have been
worn out by the activity of his foeman, suddenly seized
the mace which hung at his saddlebow, and, with a strong
hand and unerring aim, hurled it against the head of the
Emir, [2] for such and not less his enemy appeared. The
Saracen was just aware of the formidable missile in time
to interpose his light buckler betwixt the mace and his
head ; but the violence of the blow forced the buckler
down on his turban, and though that defence also con-
tributed to deaden its violence, the Saracen was beaten
from his horse. Ere the Christian could avail himself of
this mishap, his nimble foeman sprung from the ground,
and calling on his horse, which instantly returned to his
side, he leapt into his seat without touching the stirrup,
and regained all the advantage of which the Knight of
the Leopard hoped to deprive him. But the latter had
in the meanwhile recovered his mace, and the Eastern
cavalier, who remembered the strength and dexterity
with which his antagonist had aimed it, seemed to keep
cautiously out of reach of that weapon, of which he had
so lately felt the force, while he showed his purpose of
waging a distant warfare with missile weapons of his
own. Planting his long spear in the sand at a distance
from the scene of combat, he strung, with great address,

[1] That is, a tame hawk or falcon, trained to attack or capture
other birds.

[2] The title given in Mohammedan countries to an independent
chief.

a short bow, which he carried on his back, and putting his horse to the gallop, once more described two or three 235 circles of a wider extent than formerly, in the course of which he discharged six arrows at the Christian with such unerring skill that the goodness of his harness[1] alone saved him from being wounded in as many places. The seventh shaft apparently found a less perfect part 240 of the armor, and the Christian dropped heavily from his horse. But what was the surprise of the Saracen, when, dismounting to examine the condition of his prostrate enemy, he found himself suddenly within the grasp of the European, who had had recourse to this artifice to 245 bring his enemy within his reach! Even in this deadly grapple, the Saracen was saved by his agility and presence of mind. He unloosed the sword-belt, in which the Knight of the Leopard had fixed his hold, and, thus eluding his fatal grasp, mounted his horse, which seemed 250 to watch his motions with the intelligence of a human being, and again rode off. But in the last encounter the Saracen had lost his sword and his quiver of arrows, both of which were attached to the girdle, which he was obliged to abandon. He had also lost his turban in the 255 struggle. These disadvantages seemed to incline the Moslem to a truce. He approached the Christian with his right hand extended, but no longer in a menacing attitude.

"There is truce betwixt our nations," he said, in the 260 lingua franca[2] commonly used for the purpose of communication with the Crusaders; "wherefore should there be war betwixt thee and me?—Let there be peace betwixt us."

[1] Armor.

[2] Literally, free tongue (Italian); a language or dialect under-

"I am well contented," answered he of the Couchant 265 Leopard; "but what security dost thou offer that thou wilt observe the truce?"

"The word of a follower of the Prophet[1] was never broken," answered the Emir. "It is thou, brave Nazarene,[2] from whom I should demand security, did I not 270 know that treason seldom dwells with courage."

The Crusader felt that the confidence of the Moslem made him ashamed of his own doubts.

"By the cross of my sword," he said, laying his hand on the weapon as he spoke, "I will be true companion 275 to thee, Saracen, while our fortune wills that we remain in company together!"

"By Mohammed, Prophet of God, and by Allah, God of the Prophet," replied his late foeman, "there is not treachery in my heart towards thee! And now wend we 280 to yonder fountain, for the hour of rest is at hand, and the stream had hardly touched my lip when I was called to battle by thy approach."

The Knight of the Couchant Leopard yielded a ready and courteous assent; and the late foes, without an an- 285 gry look or gesture of doubt, rode side by side to the little cluster of palm-trees.

We have spoken of a moment of truce in the midst of war; and this, a spot of beauty in the midst of a sterile desert, was scarce less dear to the imagination. It 290 was a scene which perhaps would elsewhere have deserved little notice; but as the single speck in a bound-

---

stood over a wide extent of territory in which several languages may be spoken.

[1] Mohammed, or Mahomet.

[2] A contemptuous term for Christian, or follower of Jesus of Nazareth.

less horizon which promised the refreshment of shade and living water, these blessings, held cheap where they are common, rendered the fountain and its neighborhood 295 a little paradise. Some generous or charitable hand, ere yet the evil days of Palestine began, had walled in and arched over the fountain, to preserve it from being absorbed in the earth, or choked by the flitting clouds of dust with which the least breath of wind covered the des- 300 ert. The arch was now broken and partly ruinous ; but it still so far projected over, and covered in the fountain, that it excluded the sun in a great measure from its waters, which, hardly touched by a straggling beam while all around was blazing, lay in a steady repose, 305 alike delightful to the eye and the imagination. Stealing from under the arch, they were first received in a marble basin, much defaced indeed, but still cheering the eye, by showing that the place was anciently considered as a station, that the hand of man had been 310 there, and that man's accommodation had been in some measure attended to. The thirsty and weary traveller was reminded by these signs that others had suffered similar difficulties, reposed in the same spot, and doubtless found their way in safety to a more fertile country. 315 Again, the scarce visible current which escaped from the basin served to nourish the few trees which surrounded the fountain, and where it sunk into the ground and disappeared its refreshing presence was acknowledged by a carpet of velvet verdure. 320

SHERWOOD FOREST

IN THE REIGN OF RICHARD THE FIRST.

IN that pleasant district of merry England which is watered by the river Don, there extended in ancient times a large forest, covering the greater part of the beautiful hills and valleys which lie between Sheffield and the pleasant town of Doncaster. The remains of this extensive wood are still to be seen at the noble seats of Wentworth, of Wharncliffe Park, and around Rotherham. Here haunted of yore the fabulous Dragon of Wantley; here were fought many of the most desperate battles during the Civil Wars of the Roses; and here also flourished in ancient times those bands of gallant outlaws, whose deeds have been rendered so popular in English song.

Such being our chief scene, the date of our story refers to a period towards the end of the reign of Richard I., when his return from his long captivity had become an event rather wished than hoped for by his despairing subjects, who were in the meantime subjected to every species of subordinate oppression. The nobles, whose power had become exorbitant during the reign of Stephen, and whom the prudence of Henry the Second had scarce reduced into some degree of subjection to the crown, had now resumed their ancient license in its utmost extent; despising the feeble interference of the

English Council of State, fortifying their castles, increas- 25
ing the number of their dependants, reducing all around
them to a state of vassalage, and striving by every means
in their power to place themselves each at the head of
such forces as might enable him to make a figure in the 30
national convulsions which appeared to be impending.

The situation of the inferior gentry, or franklins as
they were called, who by the law and spirit of the English constitution were entitled to hold themselves independent of feudal tyranny, became now unusually preca- 35
rious. If, as was most generally the case, they placed
themselves under the protection of any of the petty
kings[1] in their vicinity, accepted of feudal offices in his
household, or bound themselves by mutual treaties of
alliance and protection to support him in his enter- 40
prises, they might indeed purchase temporary repose ;
but it must be with the sacrifice of that independence
which was so dear to every English bosom, and at the
certain hazard of being involved as a party in whatever
rash expedition the ambition of their protector might 45
lead him to undertake. On the other hand, such and
so multiplied were the means of vexation and oppression possessed by the great barons, that they never
wanted the pretext, and seldom the will, to harass and
pursue, even to the very edge of destruction, any of their 50
less powerful neighbors who attempted to separate themselves from their authority, and to trust for their protection, during the dangers of the times, to their own inof-
fensive conduct and to the laws of the land.

The power had been completely placed in the hands 55
of the Norman nobility by the event of the battle of
Hastings, and it had been used, as our histories assure

[1] The nobles, or feudal chieftains, mentioned above.

us, with no moderate hand. The whole race of Saxon
princes and nobles had been extirpated or disinherited,
with few or no exceptions ; nor were the numbers great
who possessed land in the country of their fathers, even 60
as proprietors of the second, or of yet inferior classes.
The royal policy had long been to weaken by every
means, legal or illegal, the strength of a part of the population which was justly considered as nourishing the
most inveterate antipathy to their victor. All the mon- 65
archs of the Norman race had shown the most marked
predilection for their Norman subjects ; the laws of the
chase, and many others equally unknown to the milder
and more free spirit of the Saxon constitution, had been
fixed upon the necks of the subjugated inhabitants, to 70
add weight, as it were, to the feudal chains with which
they were loaded. At court, and in the castles of the
great nobles, where the pomp and state of a court was
emulated, Norman-French was the only language employed ; in courts of law, the pleadings and judgments 75
were delivered in the same tongue. In short, French
was the language of honor, of chivalry, and even of justice, while the far more manly and expressive Anglo-
Saxon was abandoned to the use of rustics and hinds,
who knew no other. Still, however, the necessary inter- 80
course between the lords of the soil and those oppressed
inferior beings by whom that soil was cultivated occasioned the gradual formation of a dialect, compounded
betwixt the French and the Anglo-Saxon, in which they
could render themselves mutually intelligible to each 85
other ; and from this necessity arose by degrees the
structure of our present English language, in which the
speech of the victors and the vanquished have been so
happily blended together, and which has since been so

richly improved by importations from the classical lan- 90
guages and from those spoken by the Southern nations
of Europe.

The sun was setting upon one of the rich glassy glades
of that forest which we have already mentioned.   Hundreds of broad-headed, short-stemmed, wide-branched 95
oaks, which had witnessed perhaps the stately march of
the Roman soldiery,[1] flung their gnarled arms over a
thick carpet of the most delicious green sward ; in some
places they were intermingled with beeches, hollies, and
copsewood of various descriptions, so closely as totally 100
to intercept the level beams of the sinking sun ; in others
they receded from each other, forming those long sweep-
ing vistas, in the intricacy of which the eye delights to
lose itself, while imagination considers them as the paths
to yet wilder scenes of sylvan solitude.   Here the red 105
rays of the sun shot a broken and discolored light, that
partially hung upon the shattered boughs and mossy
trunks of the trees, and there they illuminated in brilliant
patches the portions of turf to which they made their
way.   A considerable open space in the midst of this 110
glade seemed formerly to have been dedicated to the
rites of Druidical[2] superstition ; for on the summit of a
hillock, so regular as to seem artificial, there still remained part of a circle of rough, unhewn stones, of large
dimensions.   Seven stood upright ; the rest had been 115
dislodged from their places, probably by the zeal of some
convert to Christianity, and lay, some prostrate near

---

[1] Referring to the time of the Roman occupation of Britain, in
the early centuries of the Christian era.

[2] Pertaining to the *Druids,* the priests of the aboriginal Britons.
See *Notes.*

their former site, and others on the side of the hill. One large stone only had found its way to the bottom, and in stopping the course of a small brook, which glided 120 smoothly round the foot of the eminence, gave by its opposition a feeble voice of murmur to the placid and elsewhere silent streamlet.

The human figures which completed this landscape were in number two, partaking in their dress and ap- 125 pearance of that wild and rustic character which belonged to the woodlands of the West-Riding [1] of Yorkshire at that early period. The eldest of these men had a stern, savage, and wild aspect. His garment was of the simplest form imaginable, being a close jacket with 130 sleeves, composed of the tanned skin of some animal, on which the hair had been originally left, but which had been worn off in so many places that it would have been difficult to distinguish from the patches that remained to what creature the fur had belonged. This primeval 135 vestment reached from the throat to the knees, and served at once all the usual purposes of body-clothing ; there was no wider opening at the collar than was necessary to admit the passage of the head, from which it may be inferred that it was put on by slipping it over 140 the head and shoulders in the manner of a modern shirt or ancient hauberk. [2] Sandals, bound with thongs made of boar's hide, protected the feet, and a roll of thin leather was twined artificially around the legs, and, ascending above the calf, left the knees bare, like those 145 of a Scottish Highlander. To make the jacket sit yet

---

[1] The county of Yorkshire is divided into three districts known as the North, East, and West *Ridings* — originally *thrithings*, or *trithings=thirds*.

[2] Coat of mail. See p. 28 above.

more close to the body, it was gathered at the middle by
a broad leathern belt, secured by a brass buckle; to one
side of which was attached a sort of scrip,[1] and to the
other a ram's horn, accoutred with a mouthpiece, for the [150]
purpose of blowing. In the same belt was stuck one
of those long, broad, sharp-pointed, and two-edged
knives, with a buck's-horn handle, which were fabricated
in the neighborhood, and bore even at this early period
the name of a Sheffield whittle.[2] The man had no cover- [155]
ing upon his head, which was only defended by his own
thick hair, matted and twisted together, and scorched
by the influence of the sun into a rusty dark-red col-
or, forming a contrast with the overgrown beard upon
his cheeks, which was rather of a yellow or amber hue. [160]
One part of his dress only remains, but it is too remarkable to be suppressed ; it was a brass ring resembling a
dog's collar, but without any opening, and soldered fast
round his neck, so loose as to form no impediment to his
breathing, yet so tight as to be incapable of being re- [165]
moved, excepting by the use of the file. On this singular
gorget[3] was engraved, in Saxon characters, an inscription of the following purport : "Gurth, the son of Beo-
wulph, is the born thrall[4] of Cedric of Rotherwood."

Beside the swineherd, for such was Gurth's occupa- [170]
tion, was seated, upon one of the fallen Druidical monuments, a person about ten years younger in appearance,
and whose dress, though resembling his companion's
in form, was of better materials and of a more fantastic

[1] Pouch, or bag ; as in *Matthew*, x. 10, etc.

[2] An old word for knife.

[3] Properly a piece of armor for the throat or neck ; here applied
to the collar just described.

[4] Serf, or bondman ; now used only as an abstract noun.

GURTH AND WAMBA IN SHERWOOD FOREST.

appearance. His jacket had been stained of a bright [175]
purple hue, upon which there had been some attempt to
paint grotesque ornaments in different colors. To the
jacket he added a short cloak, which scarcely reached
half-way down his thigh ; it was of crimson cloth, though
a good deal soiled, lined with bright yellow ; and as he [180]
could transfer it from one shoulder to the other, or at
his pleasure draw it all around him, its width, contrasted
with its want of longitude, formed a fantastic piece of
drapery. He had thin silver bracelets upon his arms,
and on his neck a collar of the same metal, bearing the [185]
inscription, " Wamba, the son of Witless, is the thrall of
Cedric of Rotherwood." This personage had the same
sort of sandals with his companion, but instead of the
roll of leather thong his legs were cased in a sort of gaiters, of which one was red and the other yellow. He [190]
was provided also with a cap, having around it more
than one bell, about the size of those attached to hawks,[1]
which jingled as he turned his head to one side or
other ; and as he seldom remained a minute in the same
posture, the sound might be considered as incessant. [195]
Around the edge of this cap was a stiff bandeau[2] of
leather, cut at the top into open work, resembling a coronet, while a prolonged bag arose from within it, and fell
down on one shoulder like an old-fashioned nightcap, or
a jelly-bag, or the head-gear of a modern hussar.[3] It [200]
was to this part of the cap that the bells were attached ;
which circumstance, as well as the shape of his head-

[1] Small bells were fastened to the tame hawks used in falconry,
to frighten the birds that were their prey.

[2] French for *band*.

[3] Light-armed horseman ; originally applied to Hungarian cavalry. For a common form of the fool's cap, see cut on page 153.

dress, and his own half-crazed, half-cunning expression
of countenance, sufficiently pointed him out as belonging to the race of domestic clowns or jesters maintained 205
in the houses of the wealthy, to help away the tedium of
those lingering hours which they were obliged to spend
within doors. He bore, like his companion, a scrip attached to his belt, but had neither horn nor knife, being
probably considered as belonging to a class whom it is 210
esteemed dangerous to intrust with edge-tools.   In place
of these, he was equipped with a sword of lath, resembling that with which Harlequin[1] operates his wonders
upon the modern stage.

The outward appearance of these two men formed 215
scarce a stronger contrast than their look and demeanor.
That of the serf or bondsman was sad and sullen ; his
aspect was bent on the ground with an appearance of
deep dejection, which might be almost construed into
apathy, had not the fire which occasionally sparkled in 220
his red eye manifested that there slumbered, under the
appearance of sullen despondency, a sense of oppression and a disposition to resistance. The looks of Wamba, on the other hand, indicated, as usual with his class,
a sort of vacant curiosity and fidgety impatience of 225
any posture of repose, together with the utmost self-sat-
isfaction respecting his own situation and the appearance which he made. The dialogue which they maintained between them was carried on in Anglo-Saxon,
which, as we said before, was universally spoken by the 230
inferior classes, excepting the Norman soldiers and the
immediate personal dependants of the great feudal nobles. But to give their conversation in the original
would convey but little information to the modern

[1] A clown, or buffoon. See *Notes.*

reader, for whose benefit we beg to offer the following [235] translation :

"The curse of St. Withold [1] upon these porkers!" said the swineherd, after blowing his horn obstreperously to collect together the scattered herd of swine, which, answering his call with notes equally melodious, made, [240] however, no haste to remove themselves from the luxurious banquet of beech-mast [2] and acorns on which they had fattened, or to forsake the marshy banks of the rivulet, where several of them, half plunged in mud, lay stretched at their ease, altogether regardless of the voice of their [245] keeper. "The curse of St. Withold upon them and upon me!" said Gurth; "if the two-legged wolf snap not up some of them ere nightfall, I am no true man. Here, Fangs! Fangs!" he ejaculated at the top of his voice to a ragged, wolfish-looking dog, a sort of lurcher, [3] [250] half mastiff, half greyhound, which ran limping about as if with the purpose of seconding his master in collecting the refractory grunters ; but which, in fact, from misapprehension of the swineherd's signals, ignorance of his own duty, or malice prepense, [4] only drove them hither [255] and thither, and increased the evil which he seemed to design to remedy. "A devil draw the teeth of him," said Gurth, "and the mother of mischief confound the Ranger of the forest, that cuts the foreclaws off our dogs and makes them unfit for their trade!" [5] Wamba, up and [260]

[1] A corruption of *St. Vitalis.*

[2] Beech-nuts.

[3] A dog that *lurches* (lurks), or lies in wait for game.

[4] Premeditated, deliberate ; rarely used except in the phrase *malice prepense.*

[5] A most sensible grievance of those aggrieved times were the Forest Laws. These oppressive enactments were the produce of the Norman Conquest, for the Saxon laws of the chase were mild

help me an' thou beest a man; take a turn round the back o' the hill to gain the wind on them; and when thou'st got the weather-gage, thou mayst drive them before thee as gently as so many innocent lambs."

"Truly," said Wamba, without stirring from the spot, 265 "I have consulted my legs upon this matter, and they are altogether of opinion that to carry my gay garments through these sloughs would be an act of unfriendship to my sovereign person and royal wardrobe; wherefore, Gurth, I advise thee to call off Fangs, and leave the 270 herd to their destiny, which, whether they meet with bands of travelling soldiers, or of outlaws, or of wandering pilgrims, can be little else than to be converted into Normans before morning, to thy no small ease and comfort."
275

"The swine turned Normans to my comfort!" quoth Gurth; "expound that to me, Wamba, for my brain is too dull and my mind too vexed to read riddles."

"Why, how call you those grunting brutes running about on their four legs?" demanded Wamba.
280

and humane; while those of William, enthusiastically attached to the exercise and its rights, were to the last degree tyrannical. The formation of the New Forest bears evidence to his passion for hunting, where he reduced many a happy village to the condition of that one commemorated by Mr. William Stewart Rose:

> "Amongst the ruins of the church
> The midnight raven found a perch,
>   A melancholy place;
> The ruthless Conqueror cast down,
> Wo worth the deed, that little town,
>   To lengthen out his chase."

The disabling dogs, which might be necessary for keeping flocks and herds from running at the deer, was called *lawing*, and was in general use (Scott).

¹ If.

"Swine, fool, swine," said the herd; "every fool knows that."

"And swine is good Saxon," said the Jester; "but how call you the sow when she is flayed, and drawn, and quartered, and hung up by the heels, like a traitor?" 285

"Pork," answered the swineherd.

"I am very glad every fool knows that too," said Wamba, "and pork, I think, is good Norman-French; and so when the brute lives, and is in the charge of a Saxon slave, she goes by her Saxon name; but becomes 290 a Norman, and is called pork, when she is carried to the Castle-hall to feast among the nobles; what dost thou think of this, friend Gurth, ha?"

"It is but too true doctrine, friend Wamba, however it got into thy fool's pate." 295

"Nay, I can tell you more," said Wamba, in the same tone; "there is old Alderman Ox continues to hold his Saxon epithet while he is under the charge of serfs and bondsmen such as thou, but becomes Beef, a fiery French gallant, when he arrives before the worshipful jaws that 300 are destined to consume him. Mynheer Calf, too, becomes Monsieur de Veau[1] in the like manner; he is Saxon when he requires tendance, and takes a Norman name when he becomes matter of enjoyment."

"A murrain[2] take thee," rejoined the swineherd; 305 "wilt thou talk of such things while a terrible storm of thunder and lightning is raging within a few miles of us? Hark, how the thunder rumbles! and for summer rain, I never saw such broad, downright, flat drops fall out of the clouds; the oaks, too, notwithstanding the 310 calm weather, sob and creak with their great boughs as

---

[1] French for *veal*, which is really the same word.

[2] Plague. See *Exodus*, ix. 3, etc.

if announcing a tempest. Thou canst play the rational
if thou wilt ; credit me for once, and let us home ere
the storm begins to rage, for the night will be fearful."

Wamba seemed to feel the force of this appeal, and 315
accompanied his companion, who began his journey after catching up a long quarter-staff[1] which lay upon the
grass beside him. This second Eumæus[2] strode hastily
down the forest glade, driving before him, with the as-
sistance of Fangs, the whole herd of his inharmonious 320
charge.

[1] An old English weapon, a stout pole about six feet and a half
long, generally loaded with iron at both ends.

[2] The faithful swineherd of Ulysses in Homer's *Odyssey*.

CRUSADERS.

THEY stood before the mansion of Cedric—a low irregular building, containing several court-yards or enclosures, extending over a considerable space of ground, and which, though its size argued the inhabitant to be a person of wealth, differed entirely from the tall, turreted, 5 and castellated buildings in which the Norman nobility resided, and which had become the universal style of architecture throughout England.

Rotherwood was not, however, without defences; no habitation in that disturbed period could have been so, 10 without the risk of being plundered and burnt before the next morning. A deep fosse, or ditch, was drawn round the whole building, and filled with water from a neighboring stream. A double stockade, or palisade, composed of pointed beams, which the adjacent forest 15 supplied, defended the outer and inner bank of the trench. There was an entrance from the west through the outer stockade, which communicated by a drawbridge with a similar opening in the interior defences. Some precautions had been taken to place those en- 20 trances under the protection of projecting angles, by which they might be flanked [1] in case of need by archers or slingers.

In a hall, the height of which was greatly dispropor-

[1] Defended from the side; a military term.

tioned to its extreme length and width, a long oaken 25
table, formed of planks rough-hewn from the forest, and
which had scarcely received any polish, stood ready
prepared for the evening meal of Cedric the Saxon. The
roof, composed of beams and rafters, had nothing to
divide the apartment from the sky excepting the plank- 30
ing and thatch;[1] there was a huge fireplace at either
end of the hall, but as the chimneys were constructed
in a very clumsy manner, at least as much of the
smoke found its way into the apartment as escaped by
the proper vent. The constant vapor which this occa- 35
sioned had polished the rafters and beams of the low-
browed[2] hall, by encrusting them with a black varnish
of soot. On the sides of the apartment hung imple-
ments of war and of the chase, and there were at each
corner folding-doors, which gave access to other parts 40
of the extensive building.

The other appointments of the mansion partook of
the rude simplicity of the Saxon period, which Cedric
piqued himself upon maintaining. The floor was composed of earth mixed with lime, trodden into a hard 45
substance, such as is often employed in flooring our
modern barns. For about one quarter of the length of
the apartment the floor was raised by a step, and this
space, which was called the dais, was occupied only by
the principal members of the family and visitors of dis- 50
tinction. For this purpose, a table richly covered with
scarlet cloth was placed transversely across the platform, from the middle of which ran the longer and lower
board, at which the domestics and inferior persons fed,

---

[1] The roof was *thatched* with straw, instead of being covered with tiles.

[2] Low-studded, as we should say.

down towards the bottom of the hall. The whole resem- 55
bled the form of the letter T, or some of those ancient
dinner-tables, which, arranged on the same principles,
may be still seen in the antique Colleges of Oxford or
Cambridge. Massive chairs and settles [1] of carved oak
were placed upon the dais, and over these seats and the 60
more elevated table was fastened a canopy of cloth,
which served in some degree to protect the dignitaries
who occupied that distinguished station from the weather, and especially from the rain, which in some places
found its way through the ill-constructed roof.   65

The walls of this upper end of the hall, as far as the
dais extended, were covered with hangings or curtains,
and upon the floor there was a carpet, both of which
were adorned with some attempts at tapestry, or embroidery, executed with brilliant or rather gaudy color- 70
ing. Over the lower range of table, the roof, as we have
noticed, had no covering ; the rough plastered walls
were left bare, and the rude earthen floor was uncar-
peted ; the board was uncovered by a cloth, and rude
massive benches supplied the place of chairs.   75

In the centre of the upper table were placed two
chairs more elevated than the rest, for the master and
mistress of the family, who presided over the scene of
hospitality, and from doing so derived their Saxon title
of honor,[2] which signifies "the Dividers of Bread."   80

To each of these chairs was added a footstool, curiously carved and inlaid with ivory, which mark of distinction was peculiar to them. One of these seats was
at present occupied by Cedric the Saxon, who, though

---

[1] Settees, or benches with backs.
[2] Both *lord* and *lady* are derived from *loaf.*

but in rank a thane,[1] or, as the Normans called him, a [85] franklin, felt, at the delay of his evening meal, an irritable impatience which might have become an alderman,[2] whether of ancient or of modern times.

It appeared, indeed, from the countenance of this proprietor, that he was of a frank but hasty and choleric [90] temper. He was not above the middle stature, but broad-shouldered, long-armed, and powerfully made, like one accustomed to endure the fatigue of war or of the chase ; his face was broad, with large blue eyes, open and frank features, fine teeth, and a well-formed head, [95] altogether expressive of that sort of good-humor which often lodges with a sudden and hasty temper. Pride and jealousy there was in his eye, for his life had been spent in asserting rights which were constantly liable to invasion ; and the prompt, fiery, and resolute disposition [100] of the man had been kept constantly upon the alert by the circumstances of his situation. His long yellow hair was equally divided on the top of his head and upon his brow, and combed down on each side to the length of his shoulders : it had but little tendency to gray, although [105] Cedric was approaching to his sixtieth year.

His dress was a tunic of forest green, furred at the throat and cuffs with what was called minever—a kind of fur inferior in quality to ermine,[3] and formed, it is believed, of the skin of the gray squirrel. This doublet[4] [110]

---

[1] An Anglo-Saxon title of honor. After the Norman Conquest thanes and barons were classed together.

[2] Alluding to the association of the name with a fondness for good living.

[3] A costly white fur, formerly worn by kings and still by judges in England.

[4] The garment was so called because made *double*, that is, lined or padded—originally for defence.

hung unbuttoned over a close dress of scarlet, which
sate tight to his body; he had breeches of the same,
but they did not reach below the lower part of the thigh,
leaving the knee exposed.   His feet had sandals of the
same fashion with the peasants, but of finer materials, 115
and secured in the front with golden clasps.   He had
bracelets of gold upon his arms, and a broad collar of
the same precious metal around his neck.   About his
waist he wore a richly-studded belt, in which was stuck
a short, straight, two-edged sword with a sharp point, so 120
disposed as to hang almost perpendicularly by his side.
Behind his seat was hung a scarlet cloth cloak lined
with fur, and a cap of the same materials richly embroidered, which completed the dress of the opulent land-
holder when he chose to go forth.   A short boar-spear, 125
with a broad and bright steel head, also reclined against
the back of his chair, which served him, when he walked
abroad, for the purposes of a staff or of a weapon, as
chance might require.

Several domestics, whose dress held various propor- 130
tions betwixt the richness of their master's and the
coarse and simple attire of Gurth the swineherd,
watched the looks and waited the commands of the
Saxon dignitary.   Two or three servants of a superior
order stood behind their master upon the dais ; the rest 135
occupied the lower part of the hall.   Other attendants
there were of a different description : two or three large
and shaggy greyhounds, such as were then employed in
hunting the stag and wolf; as many slow-hounds [1] of a
large bony breed, with thick necks, large heads, and 140
long ears ; and one or two of the smaller dogs, now

----

[1] Bloodhounds, or sleuth-hounds ; so called from *sleuth*, the track
of a deer.

called terriers, which waited with impatience the arrival
of the supper, but, with the sagacious knowledge of phys-
iognomy peculiar to their race, forbore to intrude upon
the moody silence of their master, apprehensive proba- 145
bly of a small white truncheon [1] which lay by Cedric's
trencher [2] for the purpose of repelling the advances of
his four-legged dependants. One grizzly old wolf-dog
alone, with the liberty of an indulged favorite, had
planted himself close by the chair of state, and occa- 150
sionally ventured to solicit notice by putting his large
hairy head upon his master's knee, or pushing his nose
into his hand. Even he was repelled by the stern command, "Down, Balder, down! I am not in the humor
for foolery." 155

In fact, Cedric, as we have observed, was in no very
placid state of mind. The Lady Rowena, who had been
absent to attend an evening mass at a distant church,
had but just returned, and was changing her garments
which had been wetted by the storm. There were as 160
yet no tidings of Gurth and his charge, which should
long since have been driven home from the forest; and
such was the insecurity of the period as to render it
probable that the delay might be explained by some
depredation of the outlaws, with whom the adjacent for- 165
est abounded, or by the violence of some neighboring
baron, whose consciousness of strength made him equally negligent of the laws of property. The matter was
of consequence, for great part of the domestic wealth of
the Saxon proprietors consisted in numerous herds of 170
swine, especially in forest-land, where those animals
easily found their food.

From his musing Cedric was suddenly awakened by

---

[1] Cudgel, club.　　　　　　　　　　[2] Wooden plate.

the blast of a horn, which was replied to by the clamor- 175
ous yells and barking of all the dogs in the hall, and
some twenty or thirty which were quartered in other
parts of the building. It cost some exercise of the white
truncheon, well seconded by the exertions of the domestics, to silence this canine clamor.   180

"To the gate, knaves !" said the Saxon, hastily, as
soon as the tumult was so much appeased that the dependants could hear his voice. "See what tidings that
horn tells us of—to announce, I ween,[1] some hership[2]
and robbery which has been done upon my lands."   185

Returning in less than three minutes, a warder announced, "that the prior Aymer of Jorvaulx, and the
good knight Brian de Bois-Guilbert, commander of the
valiant and venerable order of Knights Templars, with
a small retinue, requested hospitality and lodging for the 190
night, being on their way to a tournament[3] which was
to be held not far from Ashby-de-la-Zouche[4] on the second day from the present."

"Aymer, the prior Aymer?   Brian de Bois-Guilbert?"
—muttered Cedric ; "Normans both ;—but Norman or 195
Saxon, the hospitality of Rotherwood must not be im-
peached ; they are welcome, since they have chosen to
halt—more welcome would they have been to have rid-
den farther on their way.   But it were unworthy to murmur for a night's lodgings and a night's food ; in the 200
quality of guests, at least, even Normans must suppress
their insolence.   Go, Hundebert," he added, to a sort

---

[1] Think ; rarely used now except in poetry.

[2] The crime of carrying off cattle by force.

[3] A martial sport, or exercise of knights on horseback to show
their skill in arms. It is described at length farther on.

[4] A town in Leicestershire.

of major-domo [1] who stood behind him with a white
wand; "take six of the attendants, and introduce the
strangers to the guests' lodging. Look after their horses [205]
and mules, and see their train lack nothing. Let them
have change of vestments if they require it, and fire, and
water to wash, and wine and ale; and bid the cooks
add what they hastily can to our evening meal; and let
it be put on the board when those strangers are ready [210]
to share it."

The prior Aymer had taken the opportunity afforded
him of changing his riding-robe for one of yet more
costly materials, over which he wore a cope [2] curiously
embroidered. Besides the massive golden signet ring [215]
which marked his ecclesiastical dignity, his fingers, though
contrary to the canon, [3] were loaded with precious gems;
his sandals were of the finest leather which was import-
ed from Spain; his beard trimmed to as small dimensions as his order would possibly permit, and his shaven [220]
crown concealed by a scarlet cap richly embroidered.

The appearance of the Knight Templar was also
changed; and, though less studiously bedecked with ornament, his dress was as rich, and his appearance far
more commanding than that of his companion. He had [225]
exchanged his shirt of mail for an under-tunic of dark
purple silk, garnished with furs, over which flowed his
long robe of spotless white in ample folds. The eight-
pointed cross of his order was cut on the shoulder of his
mantle in black velvet. The high cap no longer invest- [230]
ed his brows, which were only shaded by short and thick
curled hair of a raven blackness, corresponding to his

---

[1] Steward. Compare line 279.
[2] A long cloak-like garment worn by priests.
[3] Ecclesiastical rule or law.

unusually swart [1] complexion. Nothing could be more
gracefully majestic than his step and manner, had they
not been marked by a predominant air of haughtiness, 235
easily acquired by the exercise of unresisted authority.
These two dignified persons were followed by their respective attendants.

Cedric rose to receive his guests with an air of dignified hospitality, and, descending from the dais, or elevat- 240
ed part of his hall, made three steps towards them, and
then awaited their approach.

"I grieve," he said, "reverend prior, that my vow
binds me to advance no farther upon this floor of my
fathers, even to receive such guests as you, and this 245
valiant knight of the Holy Temple. Let me also pray,
that you will excuse my speaking to you in my native
language, and that you will reply in the same if your
knowledge of it permits ; if not, I sufficiently understand
Norman to follow your meaning."   250

"Vows," said the abbot, "must be unloosed, worthy
franklin, or permit me rather to say, worthy thane,
though the title is antiquated. Vows are the knots
which tie us to Heaven—they are the cords which bind
the sacrifice to the horns of the altar—and are therefore, 255
as I said before, to be unloosened and discharged, unless our holy Mother Church shall pronounce the contrary. And respecting language, I willingly hold communication in that spoken by my respected grandmother,
Hilda of Middleham, who died in odor of sanctity, lit- 260
tle short, if we may presume to say so, of her glorious
namesake, the blessed Saint Hilda [2] of Whitby, God be
gracious to her soul!"

[1] Swarthy, dark.

[2] A famous female saint, who long resided in the Abbey at Whitby, on the coast of Yorkshire. See Scott's *Marmion*, canto ii.

The feast which was spread upon the board needed no apologies from the lord of the mansion. Swine's flesh, dressed in several modes, appeared on the lower part of the board, as also that of fowls, deer, goats, and hares, and various kinds of fish, together with huge loaves and cakes of bread, and sundry confections made of fruits and honey. The smaller sorts of wild-fowl, of which there was abundance, were not served up in platters, but brought in upon small wooden spits or broaches, and offered by the pages and domestics who bore them to each guest in succession, who cut from them such a portion as he pleased. Beside each person of rank was placed a goblet of silver ; the lower board was accommodated with large drinking-horns.[1]

When the repast was about to commence, the major-domo, or steward, suddenly raising his wand, said aloud, " Forbear !—Place for the Lady Rowena." A side-door at the upper end of the hall now opened behind the banquet-table, and Rowena, followed by four female attendants, entered the apartment. Cedric, though surprised, and perhaps not altogether agreeably so, at his ward appearing in public on this occasion, hastened to meet her, and to conduct her with respectful ceremony to the elevated seat at his own right hand, appropriated to the lady of the mansion. All stood up to receive her ; and, replying to their courtesy by a mute gesture of salutation, she moved gracefully forward to assume her place at the board. Brian de Bois-Guilbert kept his eyes riveted on the Saxon beauty, more striking perhaps to his imagination because differing widely from that of the Eastern sultanas.

Formed in the best proportions of her sex, Rowena

[1] These cups were actually made of the horns of animals.

was tall in stature, yet not so much so as to attract observation on account of superior height. Her complexion was exquisitely fair, but the noble cast of her head and features prevented the insipidity which sometimes attaches to fair beauties. Her clear blue eye, which 300 sate enshrined beneath a graceful eyebrow of brown, sufficiently marked to give expression to the forehead, seemed capable to kindle as well as melt, to command as well as to beseech. If mildness were the more natural expression of such a combination of features, it was plain 305 that in the present instance the exercise of habitual superiority and the reception of general homage had given to the Saxon lady a loftier character, which mingled with and qualified that bestowed by nature. Her profuse hair, of a color betwixt brown and flaxen, was 310 arranged in a fanciful and graceful manner in numerous ringlets, to form which art had probably aided nature. These locks were braided with gems, and, being worn at full length, intimated the noble birth and free-born condition of the maiden. A golden chain, to which was 315 attached a small reliquary[1] of the same metal, hung round her neck. She wore bracelets on her arms, which were bare. Her dress was an under-gown and kirtle[2] of pale sea-green silk, over which hung a long, loose robe which reached to the ground, having very wide sleeves, which 320 came down, however, very little below the elbow. This robe was crimson, and manufactured out of the very finest wool. A veil of silk, interwoven with gold, was attached to the upper part of it, which could be, at the wearer's pleasure, either drawn over the face and bosom 325

---

[1] Casket for holding relics.
[2] Here apparently a jacket or upper garment. It often means a skirt, or petticoat.

after the Spanish fashion, or disposed as a sort of drapery round the shoulders.

When Rowena perceived the Knight Templar's eyes bent on her with an ardor that, compared with the dark caverns under which they moved, gave them the effect of [330] lighted charcoal, she drew with dignity the veil around her face, as an intimation that the determined freedom of his glance was disagreeable. Cedric saw the motion and its cause. "Sir Templar," said he, "the cheeks of our Saxon maidens have seen too little of the sun to en- [335] able them to bear the fixed glance of a crusader."

"If I have offended," replied Sir Brian, "I crave your pardon—that is, I crave the Lady Rowena's pardon—for my humility will carry me no lower."

"The Lady Rowena," said the prior, "has punished [340] us all in chastising the boldness of my friend. Let me hope she will be less cruel to the splendid train which are to meet at the tournament."

THE scene was singularly romantic. On the verge of a wood, which approached to within a mile of the town of Ashby, was an extensive meadow of the finest and most beautiful green turf, surrounded on one side by the forest, and fringed on the other by straggling oak-trees, [5] some of which had grown to an immense size. The ground, as if fashioned on purpose for the martial display which was intended, sloped gradually down on all sides to a level bottom, which was enclosed for the lists [1] with strong palisades, forming a space of a quarter of a [10] mile in length, and about half as broad. The form of the enclosure was an oblong square, save that the corners were considerably rounded off, in order to afford more convenience for the spectators. The openings for the entry of the combatants were at the northern and [15] southern extremities of the lists, accessible by strong wooden gates, each wide enough to admit two horsemen riding abreast. At each of these portals were stationed two heralds, attended by six trumpets, as many pursuivants, and a strong body of men-at-arms for maintain- [20] ing order and ascertaining the quality of the knights who proposed to engage in this martial game.

On a platform beyond the southern entrance, formed by a natural elevation of the ground, were pitched five

[1] The enclosure within which the knightly sports were performed.

magnificent pavilions, adorned with pennons of russet [25] and black, the chosen colors of the five knights-challengers. The cords of the tents were of the same color. Before each pavilion was suspended the shield of the knight by whom it was occupied, and beside it stood his squire, quaintly disguised as a salvage [1] or sylvan [30] man, or in some other fantastic dress, according to the taste of his master and the character he was pleased to assume during the game. The central pavilion, as the place of honor, had been assigned to Brian de Bois-Guilbert, whose renown in all games of chivalry, no less than [35] his connection with the knights who had undertaken this passage of arms, had occasioned him to be eagerly received into the company of the challengers, and even adopted as their chief and leader, though he had so recently joined them. On one side of his tent were [40] pitched those of Reginald Front-de-Bœuf and Richard de Malvoisin, and on the other was the pavilion of Hugh de Grantmesnil, a noble baron in the vicinity, whose ancestor had been Lord High-Steward of England in the time of the Conqueror and his son William Rufus. [45] Ralph de Vipont, a knight of St. John of Jerusalem, who had some ancient possessions at a place called Heather, near Ashby-de-la-Zouche, occupied the fifth pavilion. From the entrance into the lists a gently sloping passage, ten yards in breadth, led up to the platform on [50] which the tents were pitched. It was strongly secured by a palisade on each side, as was the esplanade in front of the pavilions, and the whole was guarded by men-at-arms.

The northern access to the lists terminated in a simi- [55] lar entrance of thirty feet in breadth, at the extremity of

---

[1] An old form of *savage.*

which was a large enclosed space for such knights as
might be disposed to enter the lists with the challengers,
behind which were placed tents containing refreshments
of every kind for their accommodation, with armorers, 60
farriers, and other attendants, in readiness to give their
services wherever they might be necessary. '

The exterior of the lists was in part occupied by temporary galleries, spread with tapestry and carpets, and
accommodated with cushions for the convenience of 65
those ladies and nobles who were expected to attend
the tournament. A narrow space betwixt these galleries
and the lists gave accommodation for yeomanry ' and
spectators of a better degree than the mere vulgar, and
might be compared to the pit of a theatre. The pro- 70
miscuous multitude arranged themselves upon the large
banks of turf prepared for the purpose, which, aided by
the natural elevation of the ground, enabled them to over-
look the galleries, and obtain a fair view into the lists.
Besides the accommodation which these stations afforded, 75
many hundreds had perched themselves on the branches
of the trees which surrounded the meadow ; and even
the steeple of a country church at some distance was
crowded with spectators.

It only remains to notice respecting the general ar- 80
rangement, that one gallery in the very centre of the
eastern side of the lists, and consequently exactly opposite to the spot where the shock of the combat was to
take place, was raised higher than the others, more richly
decorated, and graced by a sort of throne and canopy, 85
on which the royal arms were emblazoned. Squires,
pages, and yeomen in rich liveries waited around this

---

¹ The class ranking between gentlemen and laborers ; small land-
ed proprietors.

place of honor, which was designed for Prince John and his attendants. Opposite to this royal gallery was another, elevated to the same height, on the western side of the lists; and more gayly if less sumptuously decorated than that destined for the prince himself. A train of pages and of young maidens, the most beautiful who could be selected, gayly dressed in fancy habits of green and pink, surrounded a throne decorated in the same colors. Among pennons and flags bearing wounded hearts, burning hearts, bleeding hearts, bows and quivers, and all the commonplace emblems of the triumphs of Cupid, a blazoned inscription informed the spectators that this seat of honor was designed for *La Royne de la Beaulté et des Amours.*[1] But who was to represent the Queen of Beauty and of Love on the present occasion no one was prepared to guess.

Meanwhile, spectators of every description thronged forward to occupy their respective stations, and not without many quarrels concerning those which they were entitled to hold. Some of these were settled by the men-at-arms with brief ceremony; the shafts of their battle-axes and pummels of their swords being readily employed as arguments to convince the more refractory. Others, which involved the rival claims of more elevated persons, were determined by the heralds, or by the two marshals of the field, William de Wyvil and Stephen de Martival, who, armed at all points, rode up and down the lists to enforce and preserve good order among the spectators.

Gradually the galleries became filled with knights and

---

[1] This is old French for "The Queen of Beauty and Love." In modern French *Royne* would be *Reine,* and *Beaulté* would be *Beauté.*

5

nobles in their robes of peace, whose long and rich-tinted mantles were contrasted with the gayer and more splendid habits of the ladies, who, in a greater proportion [120] than even the men themselves, thronged to witness a sport which one would have thought too bloody and dangerous to afford their sex much pleasure. The lower and interior space was soon filled by substantial yeomen and burghers, and such of the lesser gentry as, from [125] modesty, poverty, or dubious title, durst not assume any higher place. It was of course among these that the most frequent disputes for precedence occurred.

"Dog of an unbeliever," said an old man, whose thread-bare tunic bore witness to his poverty, as his sword, and [130] dagger, and golden chain intimated his pretensions to rank,—" whelp of a she-wolf! darest thou press upon a Christian, and a Norman gentleman of the blood of Montdidier ?"

This rough expostulation was addressed to Isaac [the [135] Jew], who, richly and even magnificently dressed in a gaberdine [1] ornamented with lace and lined with fur, was endeavoring to make place in the foremost row beneath the gallery for his daughter, the beautiful Rebecca, who had joined him at Ashby, and who was now [140] hanging on her father's arm, not a little terrified by the popular displeasure which seemed generally excited by her parent's presumption. But Isaac, though sufficiently timid on other occasions, knew well that at present he had nothing to fear. It was not in places of general re- [145] sort, or where their equals were assembled, that any avaricious or malevolent noble durst offer him injury. At such meetings the Jews were under the protection of the general law ; and if that proved a weak assurance,

———
[1] A loose frock.

it usually happened that there were among the persons 150
assembled some barons who, for their own interested
motives, were ready to act as their protectors.

In his joyous caracole[1] round the lists, the attention
of the prince was called by the commotion which had
attended the ambitious movement of Isaac towards the 155
higher places of the assembly. The quick eye of Prince
John instantly recognized the Jew, but was much more
agreeably attracted by the beautiful daughter of Zion,
who, terrified by the tumult, clung close to the arm of
her aged father. 160

The figure of Rebecca might indeed have compared
with the proudest beauties of England, even though it
had been judged by as shrewd a connoisseur[2] as Prince
John. Her form was exquisitely symmetrical, and was
shown to advantage by a sort of Eastern dress, which 165
she wore according to the fashion of the females of her
nation. Her turban of yellow silk suited well with the
darkness of her complexion. The brilliancy of her eyes,
the superb arch of her eyebrows, her well-formed aqui-
line nose, her teeth as white as pearl, and the pro- 170
fusion of her sable tresses, which, each arranged in its
own little spiral of twisted curls, fell down upon as
much of a lovely neck as a simarre[3] of the richest
Persian silk, exhibiting flowers in their natural colors
embossed upon a purple ground, permitted to be 175
visible—all these constituted a combination of loveli-
ness which yielded not to the most beautiful of the
maidens who surrounded her. Of the golden and pearl-

---

[1] A half-turn of a horseman to right or left.

[2] Critical judge.

[3] A light and loose garment; also spelt *simar, simare, cimar, cy-
mar,* and *chimmar.*

studded clasps which closed her vest from the throat
to the waist, the three uppermost were left unfastened 180
on account of the heat. A diamond necklace, with
pendants of inestimable value, was by this means made
more conspicuous. The feather of an ostrich, fastened
in her turban by an agraffe[1] set with brilliants, was
another distinction of the beautiful Jewess, scoffed 185
and sneered at by proud dames who sat above her,
but secretly envied by those who affected to deride
them.

[*The Jew and his daughter obtain places in front of the
lower ring, and Prince John gives signal to the heralds to
proclaim the laws of the Tournament.*]

First, the five challengers were to undertake[2] all
comers.   190

Secondly, any knight proposing to combat, might, if
he pleased, select a special antagonist from among the
challengers by touching his shield. If he did so with
the reverse of his lance, the trial of skill was made with
what were called the arms of courtesy, that is, with lances 195
at whose extremity a piece of round flat board was fixed,
so that no danger was encountered save from the shock
of the horses and riders. But if the shield was touched
with the sharp end of the lance, the combat was understood to be at *outrance ;*[3] that is, the knights were to fight 200
with sharp weapons, as in actual battle.

Thirdly, when the knights present had accomplished
their vow, by each of them breaking five lances, the
prince was to declare the victor in the first day's tour-

---

[1] Clasp (French *agrafe*).

[2] That is, to meet or encounter.

[3] The French *à outrance* (often incorrectly given *à l'outrance*), or
"to the bitter end."

ney, who should receive as prize a war-horse of exquisite 205
beauty and matchless strength; and in addition to this
reward of valor, it was now declared that he should have
the peculiar honor of naming the Queen of Love and
Beauty.

The lists now presented a most splendid spectacle. 210
The sloping galleries were crowded with all that was
noble, great, wealthy, and beautiful in the northern and
midland parts of England; and the contrast of the various dresses of these dignified spectators rendered the
view as gay as it was rich, while the interior and lower 215
space, filled with the substantial burgesses[1] and yeomen
of merry England, formed, in their more plain attire, a
dark fringe or border around this circle of brilliant embroidery, relieving and, at the same time, setting off its
splendor.   220

The heralds finished their proclamation with their
usual cry of "Largesse, largesse,[2] gallant knights!" and
gold and silver pieces were showered on them from the
galleries, it being a high point of chivalry to exhibit
liberality towards those whom the age accounted at 225
once the secretaries and the historians of honor. The
bounty of the spectators was acknowledged by the cus-
tomary shouts of "Love of Ladies—Death of Champions—Honor to the Generous—Glory to the Brave!"—
to which the more humble spectators added their accla- 230
mations, and a numerous band of trumpeters the flourish of their martial instruments. When these sounds
had ceased, the heralds withdrew from the lists in gay
and glittering procession, and none remained within

---

[1] Citizens or freemen of a *borough*, or walled town.
[2] "The cry with which heralds acknowledged the gifts of the
knights" (Scott). It is the French form of our *largess*.

them save the marshals of the field, who, armed cap-a- 235
pie,[1] sat on horseback, motionless as statues, at the opposite ends of the lists. Meantime, the enclosed space
at the northern extremity of the lists, large as it was,
was now completely crowded with knights desirous to
prove their skill against the challengers, and, when 240
viewed from the galleries, presented the appearance of
a sea of waving plumage, intermixed with glistening hel-
mets and tall lances to the extremities of which were,
in many cases, attached small pennons of about a span's
breadth, which, fluttering in the air as the breeze caught 245
them, joined with the restless motion of the feathers to
add liveliness to the scene.

At length the barriers were opened, and five knights,
chosen by lot, advanced slowly into the area; a single
champion riding in front, and the other four following 250
in pairs. All were splendidly armed, and my Saxon authority (in the Wardour Manuscript) records at great
length their devices, their colors, and the embroidery
of their horse-trappings. It is unnecessary to be particular on these subjects. To borrow lines from a con- 255
temporary poet,[2] who has written but too little:

> " The knights are dust
> And their good swords are rust,
> Their souls are with the saints, we trust."

Their escutcheons[3] have long mouldered from the walls
of their castles. Their castles themselves are but green
mounds and shattered ruins—the place that once knew
them knows them no more—nay, many a race since 260
theirs has died out and been forgotten in the very land

---

[1] From head to foot (old French).
[2] Samuel Taylor Coleridge (1772–1834).
[3] Family shields, or coats-of-arms.

which they occupied with all the authority of feudal proprietors and feudal lords. What then would it avail
the reader to know their names, or the evanescent sym-
bols of their martial rank? 265

Now, however, no whit[1] anticipating the oblivion which
awaited their names and feats, the champions advanced
through the lists, restraining their fiery steeds, and com-
pelling them to move slowly, while at the same time
they exhibited their paces, together with the grace and 270
dexterity of the riders. As the procession entered the
lists, the sound of a wild barbaric music was heard from
behind the tents of the challengers, where the perform-
ers were concealed. It was of Eastern origin, having
been brought from the Holy Land; and the mixture of 275
the cymbals and bells seemed to bid welcome at once
and defiance to the knights as they advanced. With
the eyes of an immense concourse of spectators fixed
upon them, the five knights advanced up the platform
upon which the tents of the challengers stood, and there 280
separating themselves, each touched slightly, and with
the reverse of his lance, the shield of the antagonist to
whom he wished to oppose himself. The lower orders
of spectators in general—nay, many of the higher class,
and it is even said several of the ladies, were rather dis- 285
appointed at the champions choosing the arms of courtesy. For the same sort of persons who, in the present
day, applaud most highly the deepest tragedies, were
then interested in a tournament exactly in proportion
to the danger incurred by the champions engaged. 290

Having intimated their more pacific purpose, the champions retreated to the extremity of the lists, where they
remained drawn up in a line; while the challengers, sal-

---

[1] Not at all, by no means.

lying each from his pavilion, mounted their horses, and, headed by Brian de Bois - Guilbert, descended ²⁹⁵ from the platform, and opposed themselves individually to the knights who had touched their respective shields.

At the flourish of clarions and trumpets, they started out against each other at full gallop ; and such was the ³⁰⁰ superior dexterity or good - fortune of the challengers that those opposed to Bois-Guilbert, Malvoisin, and Front-de-Bœuf, rolled on the ground. The antagonist of Grant-mesnil, instead of bearing his lance-point fair against the crest or the shield of his enemy, swerved so much from ³⁰⁵ the direct line as to break the weapon athwart¹ the person of his opponent—a circumstance which was accounted more disgraceful than that of being actually unhorsed; because the latter might happen from accident, whereas the former evinced awkwardness and want of manage- ³¹⁰ ment of the weapon and of the horse. The fifth knight alone maintained the honor of his party, and parted fairly with the Knight of St. John, both splintering their lances without advantage on either side.

The shouts of the multitude, together with the accla- ³¹⁵ mations of the heralds and the clangor of the trumpets, announced the triumph of the victors and the defeat of the vanquished. The former retreated to their pavilions, and the latter, gathering themselves up as they could, withdrew from the lists in disgrace and dejection, to ³²⁰ agree with their victors concerning the redemption of their arms and their horses, which, according to the laws of the tournament, they had forfeited. The fifth of their number alone tarried in the lists long enough to be greet-ed by the applauses of the spectators, among whom he ³²⁵

¹ Crosswise.

retreated, to the aggravation, doubtless, of his companions' mortification.

A second and a third party of knights took the field; and although they had various success, yet, upon the whole, the advantage decidedly remained with the challengers, not one of whom lost his seat or swerved from his charge—misfortunes which befell one or two of their antagonists in each encounter. The spirits, therefore, of those opposed to them seemed to be considerably damped by their continued success. Three knights only appeared on the fourth entry, who, avoiding the shields of Bois-Guilbert and Front-de-Bœuf, contented themselves with touching those of the three other knights who had not altogether manifested the same strength and dexterity. This politic selection did not alter the fortune of the field; the challengers were still successful: one of their antagonists was overthrown, and both the others failed in the *attaint*, that is, in striking the helmet and shield of their antagonist firmly and strongly, with the lance held in a direct line, so that the weapon might break unless the champion was overthrown.

After this fourth encounter there was a considerable pause; nor did it appear that any one was very desirous of renewing the contest. The spectators murmured among themselves; for, among the challengers, Malvoisin and Front-de-Bœuf were unpopular from their characters, and the others, except Grantmesnil, were disliked as strangers and foreigners.

But none shared the general feeling of dissatisfaction so keenly as Cedric the Saxon, who saw in each advantage gained by the Norman challengers a repeated triumph over the honor of England. His own education had taught him no skill in the games of chivalry, although,

with the arms of his Saxon ancestors, he had manifested
himself on many occasions a brave and determined sol- 360
dier.

At length, as the Saracenic music of the challengers
concluded one of those long and high flourishes with
which they had broken the silence of the lists, it was answered by a solitary trumpet, which breathed a note of 365
defiance from the northern extremity. All eyes were
turned to see the new champion which these sounds announced, and no sooner were the barriers opened than
he paced into the lists. As far as could be judged of a
man sheathed in armor, the new adventurer did not 370
greatly exceed the middle size, and seemed to be rather
slender than strongly made. His suit of armor was
formed of steel, richly inlaid[1] with gold, and the device
on his shield was a young oak-tree pulled up by the
roots, with the Spanish word *Desdichado*, signifying Dis- 375
inherited. He was mounted on a gallant black horse,
and as he passed through the lists he gracefully saluted
the prince and the ladies by lowering his lance. The
dexterity with which he managed his steed, and something of youthful grace which he displayed in his manner, 380
won him the favor of the multitude, which some of the
lower classes expressed by calling out, "Touch Ralph
de Vipont's shield — touch the Hospitaller's[2] shield ;
he has the least sure seat, he is your cheapest bar-
gain."   385

The champion, moving onward amid these well-meant
hints, ascended the platform by the sloping alley which

---

[1] Many fine specimens of armor thus inlaid with gold may be
seen in the Tower of London and other foreign collections.

[2] The *Hospitallers* were an order of knights who built a hospital
for pilgrims at Jerusalem in the year 1042.

led to it from the lists, and to the astonishment of all
present, riding straight up to the central pavilion, struck
with the sharp end of his spear the shield of Brian de 390
Bois-Guilbert until it rung again. All stood astonished
at his presumption, but none more than the redoubted
knight whom he had thus defied to mortal combat, and
who, little expecting so rude a challenge, was standing
carelessly at the door of the pavilion. 395

" Have you confessed yourself, brother," said the Templar, " and have you heard mass this morning, that you
peril your life so frankly?"

" I am fitter to meet death than thou art," answered the Disinherited Knight ; for by this name the 400
stranger had recorded himself in the books of the
tourney.

" Then take your place in the lists," said Bois-Guilbert, " and look your last upon the sun ; for this night
thou shalt sleep in Paradise." 405

" Gramercy¹ for thy courtesy," replied the Disinherited Knight ; " and to requite it, I advise thee to take a
fresh horse and a new lance, for by my honor you will
need both."

Having expressed himself thus confidently, he reined 410
his horse backward down the slope which he had ascended, and compelled him in the same manner to move
backward through the lists till he reached the northern
extremity, where he remained stationary, in expectation
of his antagonist. This feat of horsemanship again at- 415
tracted the applause of the multitude.

However incensed at his adversary for the precautions
which he recommended, Brian de Bois-Guilbert did not
neglect his advice ; for his honor was too nearly con-

¹ Great thanks ; a corruption of the French *grand merci.*

cerned to permit his neglecting any means which might [420]
insure victory over his presumptuous opponent.   He
changed his horse for a proved and fresh one of great
strength and spirit.   He chose a new and a tough spear,
lest the wood of the former might have been strained in
the previous encounters he had sustained.   Lastly, he [425]
laid aside his shield, which had received some little damage, and received another from his squires.   His first
had only borne the general device of his rider, represent-
ing two knights riding upon one horse, an emblem expressive of the original humility and poverty of the Tem- [430]
plars, qualities which they had since exchanged for the
arrogance and wealth that finally occasioned their suppression.   Bois-Guilbert's new shield bore a raven in
full flight, holding in its claws a skull, and bearing the
motto, *Gare le Corbeau.*[1]   [435]

When the two champions stood opposed to each
other at the two extremities of the lists, the public expectation was strained to the highest pitch.   Few augured the possibility that the encounter could terminate
well for the Disinherited Knight, yet his courage and [440]
gallantry secured the general good wishes of the spectators.

The trumpets had no sooner given the signal than the
champions vanished from their posts with the speed of
lightning, and closed in the centre of the lists with the [445]
shock of a thunderbolt.   The lances burst into shivers
up to the very grasp, and it seemed at the moment that
both knights had fallen, for the shock had made each
horse recoil backwards upon its haunches.   The address
of the riders recovered their steeds by use of the bridle [450]
and spur ; and having glared on each other for an in-

[1] Beware the Raven (French).

stant with eyes which seemed to flash fire through the
bars of their visors, each made a demi-volte,[1] and, retiring to the extremity of the lists, received a fresh lance
from the attendants.   455

A loud shout from the spectators, waving of scarfs
and handkerchiefs, and general acclamations, attested
the interest taken by the spectators in this encounter;
the most equal, as well as the best performed, which had
graced the day. But no sooner had the knights resumed 460
their station than the clamor of applause was hushed
into a silence so deep and so dead that it seemed the
multitude were afraid even to breathe.

A few minutes' pause having been allowed, that the
combatants and their horses might recover breath, Prince 465
John with his truncheon signed to the trumpets to sound
the onset. The champions a second time sprung from
their stations, and closed in the centre of the lists with
the same speed, the same dexterity, the same violence,
but not the same equal fortune as before.   470

In this second encounter the Templar aimed at the
centre of his antagonist's shield, and struck it so fair
and forcibly that his spear went to shivers, and the Disinherited Knight reeled in his saddle. On the other
hand, that champion had in the beginning of his career 475
directed the point of his lance towards Bois-Guilbert's
shield, but, changing his aim almost in the moment of
encounter, he addressed it to the helmet, a mark more
difficult to hit, but which, if attained, rendered the shock
more irresistible. Fair and true he hit the Norman on 480
the visor, where his lance's point kept hold of the bars.
Yet, even at this disadvantage, the Templar sustained

---

[1] A movement of the horse in which he raises his fore-feet in a
particular manner.

his high reputation ; and had not the girths of his saddle burst, he might not have been unhorsed.   As it chanced, however, saddle, horse, and man rolled on the ground 485 under a cloud of dust.

To extricate himself from the stirrups and fallen steed was to the Templar scarce the work of a moment ; and, stung with madness, both at his disgrace and at the ac- clamations with which it was hailed by the spectators, he 490 drew his sword and waved it in defiance of his conqueror. The Disinherited Knight sprung from his steed, and also unsheathed his sword.   The marshals of the field, how- ever, spurred their horses between them, and reminded them that the laws of the tournament did not, on the 495 present occasion, permit this species of encounter.

"We shall meet again, I trust," said the Templar, casting a resentful glance at his antagonist ; "and where there are none to separate us."

"If we do not," said the Disinherited Knight, "the 500 fault shall not be mine.   On foot or horseback, with spear, with axe, or with sword, I am alike ready to en- counter thee."

More and angrier words would have been exchanged, but the marshals, crossing their lances betwixt them, 505 compelled them to separate.   The Disinherited Knight returned to his first station, and Bois-Guilbert to his tent, where he remained for the rest of the day in an agony of despair.

Without alighting from his horse, the conqueror called 510 for a bowl of wine, and opening the beaver, or lower part of his helmet, announced that he quaffed it, "To all true English hearts, and to the confusion of foreign ty- rants."   He then commanded his trumpet to sound a defiance to the challengers, and desired a herald to an- 515 nounce to them that he should make no election, but was willing to encounter them in the order in which they pleased to advance against him.

The gigantic Front-de-Bœuf, armed in sable armor, was the first who took the field. He bore on a white shield a black bull's head,[1] half defaced by the numerous encounters which he had undergone, and bearing the arrogant motto, *Cave, adsum.*[2] Over this champion the Disinherited Knight obtained a slight but decisive advantage. Both knights broke their lances fairly, but Front-de-Bœuf, who lost a stirrup in the encounter, was adjudged to have the disadvantage.

In the stranger's third encounter with Sir Philip Malvoisin he was equally successful, striking that baron so forcibly on the casque that the laces of the helmet broke, and Malvoisin, only saved from falling by being unhelmeted, was declared vanquished like his companions.

In his fourth combat with De Grantmesnil, the Disinherited Knight showed as much courtesy as he had hitherto evinced courage and dexterity. De Grantmesnil's horse, which was young and violent, reared and plunged in the course of the career so as to disturb the rider's aim, and the stranger, declining to take the advantage which this accident afforded him, raised his lance, and passing his antagonist without touching him, wheeled his horse and rode back again to his own end of the lists, offering his antagonist, by a herald, the chance of a second encounter. This De Grantmesnil declined, avowing himself vanquished as much by the courtesy as by the address of his opponent.

---

[1] As a symbol of his name, which means *Bull's head.*

[2] Beware; I am here (Latin).

Ralph de Vipont summed up the list of the stranger's triumphs, being hurled to the ground with such force that the blood gushed from his nose and his mouth, and he was borne senseless from the lists.   550

The acclamations of thousands applauded the unanimous award of the prince and marshals, announcing that day's honors to the Disinherited Knight.

The prince made a sign with his truncheon as the knight passed him in his career around the lists.   The 555 knight turned towards the throne, and, sinking his lance until the point was within a foot of the ground, remained motionless, as if expecting John's commands; while all admired the sudden dexterity with which he instantly reduced his fiery steed from a state of violent emotion 560 and high excitation to the stillness of an equestrian statue.

"Sir Disinherited Knight," said Prince John, "since that is the only title by which we can address you, it is now your duty, as well as privilege, to name the fair lady 565 who, as Queen of Honor and of Love, is to preside over next day's festival. If, as a stranger in our land, you should require the aid of other judgment to guide your own, we can only say that Alicia, the daughter of our gallant knight Waldemar Fitzurse, has at our court been 570 long held the first in beauty as in place.   Nevertheless, it is your undoubted prerogative to confer on whom you please this crown, by the delivery of which to the lady of your choice, the election of to-morrow's Queen will be formal and complete.   Raise your lance."   575

The knight obeyed; and Prince John placed upon its point a coronet of green satin, having around its edge a circlet of gold, the upper edge of which was relieved

ASHBY-DE-LA-ZOUCHE CASTLE, LEICESTER.

by arrow-points and hearts placed interchangeably, like
the strawberry leaves [1] and balls upon a ducal crown.   580

The Disinherited Knight passed the gallery close to
that of the prince, in which the Lady Alicia was seated
in the full pride of triumphant beauty, and, pacing for- .
wards as slowly as he had hitherto rode swiftly around
the lists, he seemed to exercise his right of examining 585
the numerous fair faces which adorned that splendid
circle.

It was worth while to see the different conduct of the
beauties who underwent this examination during the
time it was proceeding. Some blushed, some assumed 590
an air of pride and dignity, some looked straight forward, and essayed to seem utterly unconscious of what
was going on, some drew back in alarm, which was perhaps affected, some endeavored to forbear smiling, and
there were two or three who laughed outright. There 595
were also some who dropped their veils over their
charms ; but as the Wardour Manuscript says these
were fair ones of ten years' standing, it may be supposed
that, having had their full share of such vanities, they
were willing to withdraw their claim, in order to give a 600
fair chance to the rising beauties of the age.

At length the champion paused beneath the balcony
in which the Lady Rowena was placed, and the expectation of the spectators was excited to the utmost.

Whether from indecision or some other motive of hes- 605
itation, the champion of the day remained stationary for
more than a minute, while the eyes of the silent audience
were riveted upon his motions ; and then, gradually and
gracefully sinking the point of his lance, he deposited

---

[1] The coronet of a duke has eight strawberry leaves in a circle
round the top.

the coronet which it supported at the feet of the fair 610 Rowena. The trumpets instantly sounded, while the heralds proclaimed the Lady Rowena the Queen of Beauty and of Love.

ARCHERY—ROBIN HOOD.

[Robin Hood, the " bold Outlaw," is present at the Tournament, under the name of Locksley the Yeoman.]

"THE yeomen and commons," said De Bracy, "must not be dismissed discontented, for lack of their share in the sports."

"The day," said Waldemar, "is not yet very far spent—let the archers shoot a few rounds at the target, 5 and the prize be adjudged. This will be an abundant fulfilment of the prince's promises, so far as this herd of Saxon serfs is concerned."

"I thank thee, Waldemar," said the prince; "thou remindest me, too, that I have a debt to pay to that in- 10 solent peasant who yesterday insulted our person."

The sound of the trumpets soon recalled those spectators who had already begun to leave the field; and proclamation was made that Prince John, suddenly called by high and peremptory public duties, held him- 15 self obliged to discontinue the entertainments of to-morrow's festival. Nevertheless, that, unwilling so many good yeomen should depart without a trial of skill, he was pleased to appoint them, before leaving the ground, presently to execute the competition of archery intended 20 for the morrow. To the best archer a prize was to be awarded, being a bugle-horn, mounted with silver, and a silken baldric [1] richly ornamented with a medallion of Saint Hubert, the patron of sylvan sport.

[1] Belt.

More than thirty yeomen at first presented themselves ₂₅ as competitors, several of whom were rangers [1] and under-keepers in the royal forests of Needwood and Charnwood. When, however, the archers understood with whom they were to be matched, upwards of twenty withdrew themselves from the contest, unwilling to encounter ₃₀ the dishonor of almost certain defeat. For in those days the skill of each celebrated marksman was as well known for many miles round him as the qualities of a horse trained at Newmarket are familiar to those who frequent that well-known meeting. ₃₅

The diminished list of competitors for sylvan fame still amounted to eight. Prince John stepped from his royal seat to view more nearly the persons of these chosen yeomen, several of whom wore the royal livery. Having satisfied his curiosity by this investigation, he ₄₀ looked for the object of his resentment, whom he observed standing on the same spot, and with the same composed countenance which he had exhibited upon the preceding day.

"Fellow," said Prince John, "I guessed by thy inso- ₄₅ lent babble thou wert no true lover of the long-bow, and I see thou darest not adventure thy skill among such merrymen [2] as stand yonder."

"Under favor, sir," replied the yeoman, "I have another reason for refraining to shoot, besides the fearing ₅₀ discomfiture and disgrace."

"And what is thy other reason?" said Prince John, who, for some cause which perhaps he could not himself

[1] Officers whose duty it was to walk through the forest, guard against trespassers, etc.

[2] Archers; a term often applied to the companions of Robin Hood.

have explained, felt a painful curiosity respecting this
individual.   55

"Because," replied the woodsman, "I know not if
these yeomen and I are used to shoot at the same
marks; and because, moreover, I know not how your
grace might relish the winning of a third prize by one
who has unwittingly fallen under your displeasure."   60

Prince John colored as he put the question, "What is
thy name, yeoman?"

"Locksley," answered the yeoman.

"Then, Locksley," said Prince John, "thou shalt shoot
in thy turn, when these yeomen have displayed their   65
skill. If thou carriest the prize, I will add to it twenty
nobles;[1] but if thou losest it, thou shalt be stript of thy
Lincoln green[2] and scourged out of the lists with bow-
strings, for a wordy and insolent braggart."

"And how if I refuse to shoot on such a wager?" said   70
the yeoman. "Your grace's power, supported as it is
by so many men-at-arms, may indeed easily strip and
scourge me, but cannot compel me to bend or to draw
my bow."

"If thou refusest my fair proffer," said the prince,   75
"the provost of the lists shall cut thy bowstring, break
thy bow and arrows, and expel thee from the presence
as a faint-hearted craven."

"This is no fair chance you put on me, proud prince,"
said the yeoman, "to compel me to peril myself against   80
the best archers of Leicester and Staffordshire, under
the penalty of infamy if they should overshoot me. Nevertheless, I will obey your pleasure."

---

[1] A gold coin worth ten shillings.
[2] A kind of cloth made at Lincoln, much worn by huntsmen.

A target was placed at the upper end of the southern avenue which led to the lists. The contending archers 85 took their station in turn at the bottom of the southern access, the distance between that station and the mark allowing full distance for what was called a shot at rovers. The archers, having previously determined by lot their order of precedence, were to shoot each three 90 shafts in succession. The sports were regulated by an officer of inferior rank, termed the Provost of the Games; for the high rank of the marshals of the lists would have been held degraded had they condescended to superin- tend the sports of the yeomanry.   95

One by one the archers, stepping forward, delivered their shafts yeomanlike and bravely. Of twenty-four ar- rows, shot in succession, ten were fixed in the target, and the others ranged so near it, that, considering the dis- tance of the mark, it was accounted good archery. Of 100 the ten shafts which hit the target, two within the inner ring were shot by Hubert, a forester in the service of Malvoisin, who was accordingly pronounced victorious.

"Now, Locksley," said Prince John to the bold yeo- man, with a bitter smile, "wilt thou try conclusions with 105 Hubert, or wilt thou yield up bow, baldric, and quiver to the provost of the sports?"

"Sith[1] it be no better," said Locksley, "I am content to try my fortune, on condition that when I have shot two shafts at yonder mark of Hubert's, he shall be bound 110 to shoot one at that which I shall propose."

"That is but fair," answered Prince John, "and it shall not be refused thee.—If thou dost beat this brag- gart, Hubert, I will fill the bugle with silver pennies for thee."   115

---

[1] Since; an obsolete form.

"A man can do but his best," answered Hubert;
"but my grandsire drew a good long-bow at Hastings,[1]
and I trust not to dishonor his memory."

The former target was now removed, and a fresh one
of the same size placed in its room. Hubert, who, as 120
victor in the first trial of skill, had the right to shoot
first, took his aim with great deliberation, long measur-
ing the distance with his eye, while he held in his hand
his bended bow with the arrow placed on the string.
At length he made a step forward, and raising the bow 125
at the full stretch of his left arm, till the centre or grasp-
ing-place was nigh level with his face, he drew his bow-
string to his ear. The arrow whistled through the air
and lighted within the inner ring of the target, but not
exactly in the centre.   130

"You have not allowed for the wind, Hubert," said
his antagonist, bending his bow, "or that had been a
better shot."

So saying, and without showing the least anxiety to
pause upon his aim, Locksley stept to the appointed sta- 135
tion, and shot his arrow as carelessly in appearance as
if he had not even looked at the mark. He was speaking almost at the instant that the shaft left the bow-
string, yet it alighted in the target two inches nearer to
the white spot which marked the centre than that of 140
Hubert.

Hubert resumed his place, and not neglecting the
caution which he had received from his adversary, he
made the necessary allowance for a very light air of
wind which had just arisen, and shot so successfully that 145
his arrow alighted in the very centre of the target.

"A Hubert! a Hubert!" shouted the populace, more

[1] The battle of Hastings.

interested in a known person than in a stranger. "In the clout!¹ in the clout! a Hubert forever!"

"Thou canst not mend that shot, Locksley," said the prince, with an insulting smile.

"I will notch his shaft for him, however," replied Locksley.

And letting fly his arrow with a little more precaution than before, it lighted right upon that of his competitor, which it split to shivers. The people who stood around were so astonished at his wonderful dexterity that they could not even give vent to their surprise in their usual clamor. "This must be the devil, and no man of flesh and blood," whispered the yeomen to each other; "such archery was never seen since a bow was first bent in Britain."

"And now," said Locksley, "I will crave your grace's permission to plant such a mark as is used in the North Country, and welcome every brave yeoman who shall try a shot at it to win a smile from the bonny lass he loves best."

He then turned to leave the lists. "Let your guards attend me," he said, "if you please—I go but to cut a rod from the next willow bush."

Prince John made a signal that some attendants should follow him in case of his escape; but the cry of "Shame! shame!" which burst from the multitude, induced him to alter his ungenerous purpose.

Locksley returned almost instantly with a willow-wand about six feet in length, perfectly straight, and rather thicker than a man's thumb. He began to peel this with great composure, observing at the same time, that to ask a good woodsman to shoot at a target so

¹ The white centre of the target, mentioned above.

broad as had hitherto been used was to put shame upon 180
his skill.   "For his own part," he said, "and in the land
where he was bred, men would as soon take for their
mark King Arthur's round - table, which held sixty
knights around it.   A child of seven years old," he
said, "might hit yonder target with a headless shaft ; 185
but," added he, walking deliberately to the other end
of the lists, and sticking the willow-wand upright in the
ground, " he that hits that rod at five-score yards, I call
him an archer fit to bear both bow and quiver before a
king, an it were the stout King Richard himself."   190

"My grandsire," said Hubert, "drew a good bow at
the battle of Hastings, and never shot at such a mark in
his life—and neither will I.   If this yeoman can cleave
that rod, I give him the bucklers [1]—or rather, I yield to
the devil that is in his jerkin,[2] and not to any human 195
skill ; a man can but do his best, and I will not shoot
where I am sure to miss.   I might as well shoot at the
edge of our parson's whittle,[3] or at a wheat straw, or at
a sunbeam, as at a twinkling white streak which I can
hardly see."   200

"Cowardly dog !" said Prince John.   "Sirrah Locksley, do thou shoot ; but if thou hittest such a mark, I
will say thou art the first man ever did so.   Howe'er it
be, thou shalt not crow over us with a mere show of
superior skill."   205

"I will do my best, as Hubert says," answered Locksley ; "no man can do more."

So saying, he again bent his bow, but on the present
occasion looked with attention to his weapon, and
changed the string, which he thought was no longer 210

---

[1] I give up the contest, own myself beaten.
[2] Short coat, or jacket.   [3] Knife.   See p. 42 above.

truly round, having been a little frayed by the two former
shots. He then took his aim with some deliberation, and
the multitude awaited the event in breathless silence.
The archer vindicated their opinion of his skill : his arrow split the willow rod against which it was aimed. 215
A jubilee of acclamations followed ; and even Prince
John, in admiration of Locksley's skill, lost for an instant his dislike to his person. " These twenty nobles,"
he said, " which, with the bugle, thou hast fairly won,
are thine own ; we will make them fifty if thou wilt take 220
livery and service with us as a yeoman of our body-guard,
and be near to our person. For never did so strong
a hand bend a bow, or so true an eye direct a shaft."

"Pardon me, noble prince," said Locksley ; "but
I have vowed that if ever I take service it should be 225
with your royal brother, King Richard. These twenty
nobles I leave to Hubert, who has this day drawn as
brave [1] a bow as his grandsire did at Hastings. Had
his modesty not refused the trial, he would have hit the
wand as well as I." 230

Hubert shook his head as he received with reluctance
the bounty of the stranger ; and Locksley, anxious to
escape further observation, mixed with the crowd, and
was seen no more. [2]

---

[1] Fine, excellent.

[2] Of the English archers in war Scott says elsewhere : " Of the
troops then employed, the bowmen of England were the most formidable at a distance. They were selected from the yeomen of the
country, men to whom the use of the weapon had been familiar from
childhood ; for the practice of archery was then encouraged by prizes
and public competition in every village, in order to keep up the skill
which the youth had acquired, and to extend the renown of England,
as producing the best bowmen whom the world had ever seen.

" The equipment and mode of exercise of these archers were cal-

THE SIEGE OF TORQUILSTONE.[1]

A MOMENT of peril is often also a moment of open-hearted kindness and affection. We are thrown off our guard by the general agitation of our feelings, and betray

culated to maintain their superiority. Their dress was light and had few ligatures. Instead of the numerous strings which then attached the jacket to the hose or trousers, one stout *point*, as it was called, answered the necessary purpose, without impeding the motions of the wearer. In battle the sleeve of the right arm was left open to increase the archer's agility. Each of them carried a bow and twelve arrows, or, as they termed them, 'the lives of twelve Scots,' at his girdle: their shafts had a light forked head, and were carefully adjusted so as to fly true to the aim. In using the weapon, the English archers observed a practice unknown on the Continent, drawing the bow-string, not to the breast, but to the ear, which gave a far greater command of a strong bow and long shaft. Their arrows were, accordingly, a cloth yard in length, and their bows carried to a prodigious distance. Upon the battlements of a castle, or walls of a town, the arrows fell with the rapidity of hail, and such certainty of aim as scarcely permitted a defender to show himself; nor were they less formidable when discharged against a hostile column, whether of cavalry or infantry, and whether in motion or stationary. The principal danger to which the archers were exposed was that of a rapid and determined charge of cavalry. To provide in some degree against this, each archer used to carry a wooden stake, shod with iron at both ends, the planting of which before him might in some measure afford a cover from horse. They had also swords. The stakes, however, were not always in readiness, nor were they always found effectual for the purpose, neither were their swords an adequate protection against cavalry."

[1] The castle of Front-de-Bœuf.

the intensity of those which, at more tranquil periods,
our prudence at least conceals, if it cannot altogether
suppress them.   In finding herself once more by the
side of Ivanhoe, Rebecca was astonished at the keen
sensation of pleasure which she experienced, even at a
time when all around them both was danger, if not despair.   As she felt his pulse and inquired after his
health, there was a softness in her touch and in her ac-
cents, implying a kinder interest than she would herself
have been pleased to have voluntarily expressed.   Her
voice faltered and her hand trembled, and it was only
the cold question of Ivanhoe, "Is it you, gentle maid-
en?" which recalled her to herself, and reminded her
the sensations which she felt were not and could not be
mutual.   A sigh escaped,-but it was scarce audible;
and the questions which she asked the knight concerning his state of health were put in the tone of calm
friendship.   Ivanhoe answered her hastily that he was,
in point of health, as well, and better than he could
have expected—"Thanks," he said, "dear Rebecca, to
thy helpful skill."

"He calls me *dear* Rebecca," said the maiden to herself, "but it is in the cold and careless tone which ill
suits the word.   His war-horse—his hunting hound, are
dearer to him than the despised Jewess!"

"My mind, gentle maiden," continued Ivanhoe, "is
more disturbed by anxiety than my body with pain.
From the speeches of these men who were my warders
just now, I learn that I am a prisoner, and, if I judge
aright of the loud, hoarse voice which even now despatched them hence on some military duty, I am in the
castle of Front-de-Bœuf.   If so, how will this end, or how
can I protect Rowena and my father?"

"He names not the Jew or Jewess," said Rebecca, internally; "yet what is our portion in him, and how justly am I punished by Heaven for letting my thoughts dwell upon him!" She hastened, after this brief self-accusa- 40 tion, to give Ivanhoe what information she could; but it amounted only to this, that the Templar Bois-Guilbert and the Baron Front-de-Bœuf were commanders within the castle; that it was beleaguered [1] from without, but by whom she knew not. 45

The noise within the castle, occasioned by the defensive preparations, which had been considerable for some time, now increased into tenfold bustle and clamor. The heavy yet hasty step of the men-at-arms traversed the battlements, or resounded on the narrow and wind- 50 ing passages and stairs which led to the various bartisans [2] and points of defence. The voices of the knights were heard, animating their followers or directing means of defence, while their commands were often drowned in the clashing of armor or the clamorous shouts of those 55 whom they addressed. Tremendous as these sounds were, and yet more terrible from the awful event which they presaged, there was a sublimity mixed with them which Rebecca's high-toned mind could feel even in that moment of terror. Her eye kindled, although the 60 blood fled from her cheeks; and there was a strong mixture of fear, and of a thrilling sense of the sublime, as she repeated, half whispering to herself, half speaking to her companion, the sacred text, "The quiver rattleth [3]—the glittering spear and the shield—the noise of 65 the captains and the shouting!"

But Ivanhoe was like the war-horse of that sublime

---

[1] Besieged.　　　　　　　[2] Small overhanging turrets.

[3] See *Job*, **xxxix. 23, 25**.

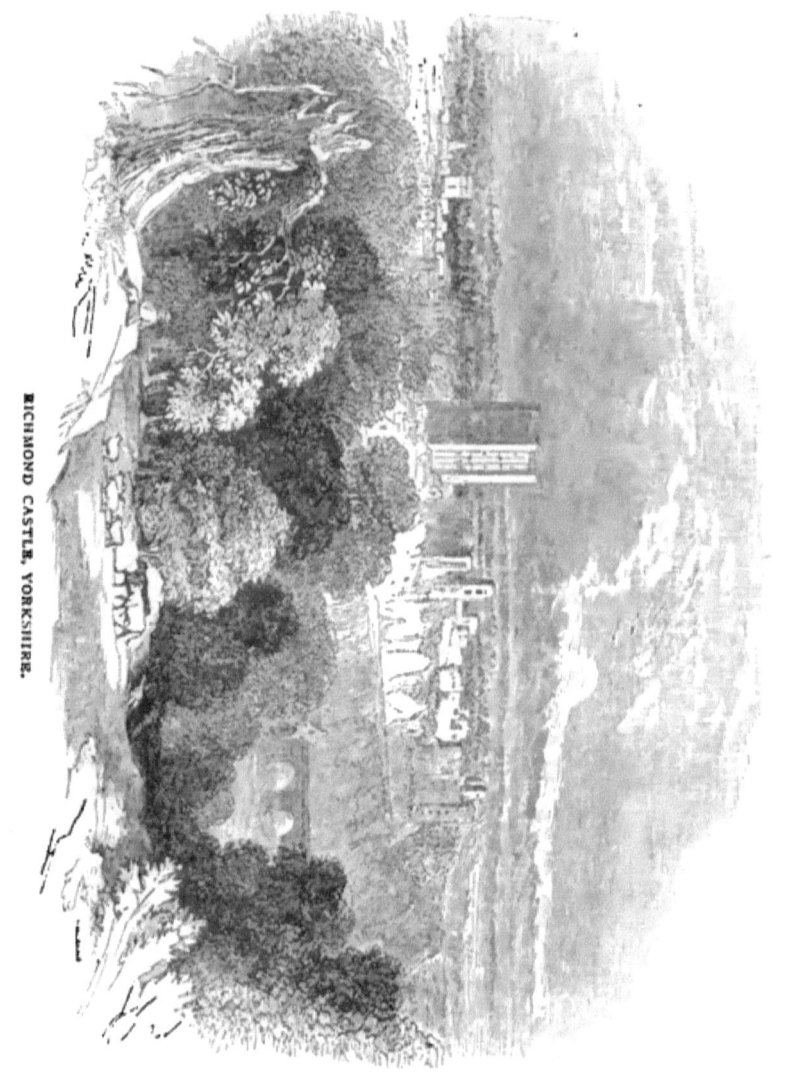

RICHMOND CASTLE, YORKSHIRE.

passage, glowing with impatience at his inactivity, and
with his ardent desire to mingle in the affray of which
these sounds were the introduction. "If I could but ₇₀
drag myself," he said, "to yonder window, that I might
see how this brave game is like to go—If I had but bow
to shoot a shaft, or battle-axe to strike were it but a
single blow for our deliverance!—It is in vain—it is in
vain—I am alike nerveless and weaponless!"   ₇₅

"Fret not thyself, noble knight," answered Rebecca,
"the sounds have ceased of a sudden—it may be they
join not battle."

"Thou knowest nought of it," said Wilfred, impa-
tiently; "this dead pause only shows that the men are ₈₀
at their posts on the walls, and expecting an instant attack; what we have heard was but the distant muttering of the storm — it will burst anon in all its fury.
Could I but reach yonder window!"

"Thou wilt but injure thyself by the attempt, noble ₈₅
knight," replied his attendant. Observing his extreme
solicitude, she firmly added, "I myself will stand at the
lattice, and describe to you as I can what passes without."

"You must not—you shall not!" exclaimed Ivanhoe;
"each lattice, each aperture, will be soon a mark for the ₉₀
archers; some random shaft—"

"It shall be welcome!" murmured Rebecca, as with
firm pace she ascended two or three steps which led to
the window of which they spoke.

"Rebecca, dear Rebecca!" exclaimed Ivanhoe, "this ₉₅
is no maiden's pastime—do not expose thyself to wounds
and death, and render me forever miserable for having
given the occasion; at least, cover thyself with yonder
ancient buckler, and show as little of your person at the
lattice as may be."   ₁₀₀

Following with wonderful **promptitude the** directions of Ivanhoe, and availing herself of the **protection** of the large ancient shield, **which she placed against the** lower part of **the window,** Rebecca, with tolerable security to herself, could **witness part of** what was passing without 105 the castle, and report to Ivanhoe the preparations which the assailants were making **for** the storm. Indeed, the **situation** which she thus obtained was peculiarly favorable **for** this purpose, because, being placed on an angle of the main building, **Rebecca** could not only see what 110 **passed** beyond the precincts of the castle, but also commanded a view of the outwork likely to be the first object of the meditated **assault.** It was an exterior fortification **of no great** height or strength, intended to protect the postern-gate [1] through which Cedric had been 115 recently **dismissed by** Front-de-Bœuf. The castle-moat divided **this species of** barbican [2] from the rest **of the** fortress, so that, in case of its being taken, it **was easy to** cut off **the communication with the main building by** withdrawing the **temporary** bridge. In the **outwork** was 120 a sallyport [3] corresponding **to the postern of the** castle, and the whole **was surrounded by a** strong palisade. Rebecca could observe, from the number of men placed **for** the defence of this post, that the besieged entertained **apprehensions** for its safety; and from the mustering of 125 the assailants in a direction nearly opposite to the outwork, **it seemed no** less plain that it had been selected as a vulnerable point of attack.

These appearances she hastily communicated to Ivanhoe, and added, "**The skirts of the wood** seem lined 130

---

[1] Small back-gate.   [2] **The** defence of an outer gate of **a** castle.

[3] A gate or underground **passage with** gates, used in making **a** sudden sally from the castle.

7

with archers, although only a few are advanced from its dark shadow."

"Under what banner?" asked Ivanhoe.

"Under no ensign of war which I can observe," answered Rebecca.   135

"A singular novelty," muttered the knight, "to advance to storm such a castle without pennon or banner displayed!—Seest thou who they be that act as leaders?"

"A knight, clad in sable armor, is the most conspicu- 140 ous," said the Jewess; "he alone is armed from head to heel, and seems to assume the direction of all around him."

"What device does he bear on his shield?" replied Ivanhoe.   145

"Something resembling a bar of iron, and a padlock painted blue on the black shield."

"A fetterlock [1] and shacklebolt [2] azure," said Ivanhoe; "I know not who may bear the device, but well I ween it might now be mine own. Canst thou not see the 150 motto?"

"Scarce the device itself at this distance," replied Rebecca; "but when the sun glances fair upon his shield, it shows as I tell you."

"Seem there no other leaders?" exclaimed the anxious 155 inquirer.

"None of mark and distinction that I can behold from this station," said Rebecca; "but doubtless the other side of the castle is also assailed. They appear even now preparing to advance — God of Zion protect 160 us!—What a dreadful sight!—Those who advance first

---

[1] Fetlock, or instrument put on a horse's leg to prevent running away.   [2] Shackle, or fetter.

bear huge shields and defences made of plank ; the others follow, bending their bows as they come on. They raise their bows !—God of Moses, forgive the creatures thou hast made !" 165

Her description was here suddenly interrupted by the signal for assault, which was given by the blast of a shrill bugle, and at once answered by a flourish of the Norman trumpets from the battlements, which, mingled with the deep and hollow clang of the nakers (a species of 170 kettle-drum), retorted in notes of defiance the challenge of the enemy. The shouts of both parties augmented the fearful din, the assailants crying, " Saint George for merry England !" [1] and the Normans answering them with cries of *"En avant* [2] *De Bracy !—Beau-seant !* 175 *Beau-seant !—Front-de-Bœuf à la rescousse !"* according to the war-cries of their different commanders.

It was not, however, by clamor that the contest was to be decided, and the desperate efforts of the assailants were met by an equally vigorous defence on the part of 180 the besieged. The archers, trained by their woodland pastimes to the most effective use of the long-bow, shot, to use the appropriate phrase of the time, so "wholly together " that no point at which a defender could show the least part of his person escaped their cloth-yard 185 shafts. [3] By this heavy discharge, which continued as thick and sharp as hail, while, notwithstanding, every arrow had its individual aim, and flew by scores together against each embrasure [4] and opening in the parapets, as

---

[1] The English battle-cry.

[2] Forward ! (French) ; as *à la rescousse !* is To the rescue !

[3] Arrows a yard long. See p. 92 (foot-note) above.

[4] An opening in a wall or parapet through which arrows or shot are fired.

well as at every window where a defender either occa- 190
sionally had post or might be suspected to be stationed,
—by this sustained discharge two or three of the garrison
were slain and several others wounded. But, confident in their armor of proof,[1] and in the cover which
their situation afforded, the followers of Front-de-Bœuf 195
and his allies showed an obstinacy in defence propor-
tioned to the fury of the attack, and replied with the
discharge of their large cross-bows, as well as with their
long-bows, slings, and other missile weapons, to the close
and continued shower of arrows ; and, as the assailants 200
were necessarily but indifferently protected, did occasionally more damage than they received at their hand.
The whizzing of shafts and of missiles on both sides was
only interruped by the shouts which arose when either
side inflicted or sustained some notable loss.   205

"And I must lie here like a bedridden monk," exclaimed Ivanhoe, "while the game that gives me freedom
or death is played out by the hand of others!—Look
from the window once again, kind maiden, but beware
that you are not marked by the archers beneath.—Look 210
out once more, and tell me if they yet advance to the
storm."

With patient courage, strengthened by the interval
which she had employed in mental devotion, Rebecca
again took post at the lattice, sheltering herself, however, 215
so as not to be visible from beneath.

"What dost thou see, Rebecca?" again demanded the
wounded knight.

"Nothing but the cloud of arrows flying so thick as
to dazzle mine eyes and to hide the bowmen who shoot 220
them."

---

[1] Impenetrability, or power of resistance in armor.

"That cannot endure," said Ivanhoe ; "if they press not right on to carry the castle by pure force of arms, the archery may avail but little against stone walls and bulwarks. Look for the Knight of the Fetterlock, fair 225 Rebecca, and see how he bears himself ; for as the leader is, so will his followers be."

"I see him not," said Rebecca.

"Foul craven !" exclaimed Ivanhoe ; "does he blench from the helm when the wind blows highest ?" 230

"He blenches not ! he blenches not !" said Rebecca, "I see him now ; he leads a body of men close under the outer barrier ¹ of the barbican.—They pull down the piles and palisades ; they hew down the barriers with axes.—His high black plume floats abroad over the 235 throng, like a raven over the field of the slain. They have made a breach in the barriers—they rush in—they are thrust back !—Front-de-Bœuf heads the defenders ; I see his gigantic form above the press. They throng again to the breach, and the pass is disputed hand to 240 hand and man to man. God of Jacob ! it is the meeting of two fierce tides—the conflict of two oceans moved by adverse winds !"

She turned her head from the lattice, as if unable longer to endure a sight so terrible. 245

"Look forth again, Rebecca," said Ivanhoe, mistaking the cause of her retiring ; "the archery must in some degree have ceased, since they are now fighting hand to hand. Look again, there is now less danger."

---

¹ "Every Gothic castle and city had, beyond the outer walls, a fortification composed of palisades, called the *barriers*, which were often the scene of severe skirmishes, as these must necessarily be carried before the walls themselves could be approached " (Scott).

Rebecca again looked forth, and almost immediate- 250
ly exclaimed, "Holy prophets of the law! Front-de-
Bœuf and the Black Knight fight hand to hand on the
breach, amid the roar of their followers, who watch the
progress of the strife — Heaven strike with the cause of
the oppressed and of the captive!" She then uttered 255
a loud shriek, and exclaimed, "He is down! — he is
down!"

"Who is down?" cried Ivanhoe; "for our dear Lady's
sake, tell me which has fallen?"

"The Black Knight," answered Rebecca, faintly; then 260
instantly again shouted with joyful eagerness—"But no
—but no!—the name of the Lord of Hosts be blessed!
—he is on foot again, and fights as if there were twenty
men's strength in his single arm. His sword is broken
—he snatches an axe from a yeoman—he presses Front- 265
de-Bœuf with blow on blow. The giant stoops and tot-
ters like an oak under the steel of the woodman—he falls
—he falls!"

"Front-de-Bœuf?" exclaimed Ivanhoe.

"Front-de-Bœuf!" answered the Jewess; "his men 270
rush to the rescue, headed by the haughty Templar—
their united force compels the champion to pause.—
They drag Front-de-Bœuf within the walls."

"The assailants have won the barriers, have they not?"
said Ivanhoe.   275

"They have—they have!" exclaimed Rebecca, "and
they press the besieged hard upon the outer wall; some
plant ladders, some swarm like bees, and endeavor to
ascend upon the shoulders of each other — down go
stones, beams, and trunks of trees upon their heads, and 280
as fast as they bear the wounded to the rear, fresh men
supply their places in the assault—Great God! hast thou

given men thine own image, that it should be thus cruelly defaced by the hands of their brethren!"

"Think not of that," said Ivanhoe; "this is no time 285 for such thoughts—Who yield?—who push their way?"

"The ladders are thrown down," replied Rebecca, shuddering; "the soldiers lie grovelling under them like crushed reptiles—the besieged have the better."

"Saint George strike for us!" exclaimed the knight; 290 "do the false yeomen give way?"

"No!" exclaimed Rebecca, "they bear themselves right yeomanly—the Black Knight approaches the postern with his huge axe—the thundering blows which he deals, you may hear them above all the din and shouts 295 of the battle—Stones and beams are hailed down on the bold champion—he regards them no more than if they were thistle-down or feathers!"

"By Saint John of Acre,"[1] said Ivanhoe, raising himself joyfully on his couch, "methought there was 300 but one man in England that might do such a deed!"

"The postern-gate shakes," continued Rebecca; "it crashes—it is splintered by his blows—they rush in—the outwork is won—O God!—they hurl the defenders from the battlements — they throw them into the moat — O 305 men, if ye be indeed men, spare them that can resist no longer!"

"The bridge—the bridge which communicates with the castle—have they won that pass?" exclaimed Ivanhoe.

"No," replied Rebecca, "the Templar has destroyed 310 the plank on which they crossed—few of the defenders escaped with him into the castle—the shrieks and cries

---

[1] The full name of this Syrian seaport is *St. Jean d'Acre*, or *St. John of Acre.* In the time of the Crusaders it became their chief landing-place and the seat of the Order of St. John.

which you hear tell the fate of the others—Alas! I see
it is still more difficult to look upon victory than upon
battle." 315

"What do they now, maiden?" said Ivanhoe; "look
forth yet again—this is no time to faint at bloodshed."

"It is over for the time," answered Rebecca; "our
friends strengthen themselves within the outwork which
they have mastered, and it affords them so good a shel- 320
ter from the foemen's shot that the garrison only be-
stow a few bolts on it from interval to interval, as if
rather to disquiet than effectually to injure them."

"Our friends," said Wilfred, "will surely not abandon
an enterprise so gloriously begun and so happily at- 325
tained—O no! I will put my faith in the good knight
whose axe hath rent heart-of-oak and bars of iron.—Singular," he again muttered to himself, "if there be two
who can do a deed of such *derring-do!*[1]—a fetterlock
and a shacklebolt on a field-sable—what may that 330
mean?—seest thou nought else, Rebecca, by which the
Black Knight may be distinguished?"

"Nothing," said the Jewess; "all about him is black
as the wing of the night-raven. Nothing can I spy that
can mark him farther—but having once seen him put 335
forth his strength in battle, methinks I could know him
again among a thousand warriors. He rushes to the
fray as if he were summoned to a banquet. There is
more than mere strength, there seems as if the whole
soul and spirit of the champion were given to every blow 340
which he deals upon his enemies. God assoilzie[2] him
of the sin of bloodshed!—it is fearful, yet magnificent,
to behold how the arm and heart of one man can triumph over hundreds."

[1] Desperate courage.   [2] Assoil, or absolve.

"Rebecca," said Ivanhoe, "thou hast painted a hero; surely they rest but to refresh their force, or to provide the means for crossing the moat. Under such a leader as thou hast spoken this knight to be, there are no craven fears, no cold-blooded delays, no yielding up a gallant emprize,[1] since the difficulties which render it arduous render it also glorious. I swear by the honor of my house—I vow by the name of my bright lady-love, I would endure ten years' captivity to fight one day by that good knight's side in such a quarrel as this!"

"Alas!" said Rebecca, leaving her station at the window, and approaching the couch of the wounded knight, "this impatient yearning after action—this struggling with and repining at your present weakness, will not fail to injure your returning health. How couldst thou hope to inflict wounds on others ere that be healed which thou thyself hast received?"

"Rebecca," he replied, "thou knowest not how impossible it is for one trained to actions of chivalry to remain passive as a priest or a woman when they are acting deeds of honor around him. The love of battle is the food upon which we live—the dust of the *mêlée* is the breath of our nostrils! We live not—we wish not to live longer than while we are victorious and renowned. Such, maiden, are the laws of chivalry to which we are sworn, and to which we offer all that we hold dear."

"Alas!" said the fair Jewess, "and what is it, valiant knight, save an offering of sacrifice to a demon of vainglory, and a passing through the fire to Moloch?[2] What remains to you as the prize of all the blood you have spilled—of all the travail and pain you have endured—

---

[1] Enterprise.
[2] See *Leviticus*, xviii. 21, 2 *Kings*, xxiii. 10, etc.

of all the tears which your deeds have caused, when
death hath broken the strong man's spear, and overtaken
the speed of his war-horse?"

"What remains?" cried Ivanhoe. "Glory, maiden,
glory! which gilds our sepulchre and embalms our name." 380

"Glory?" continued Rebecca. "Alas! is the rusted
mail which hangs as a hatchment [1] over the champion's
dim and mouldering tomb—is the defaced sculpture of
the inscription which the ignorant monk can hardly read
to the inquiring pilgrim—are these sufficient rewards for 385
the sacrifice of every kindly affection, for a life spent
miserably that ye may make others miserable? Or is
there such virtue in the rude rhymes of a wandering
bard that domestic love, kindly affection, peace and
happiness, are so wildly bartered, to become the hero of 390
those ballads which vagabond minstrels sing to drunken
churls over their evening ale?"

"By the soul of Hereward!" replied the knight impa-
tiently, "thou speakest, maiden, of thou knowest not
what. Thou wouldst quench the pure light of chivalry, 395
which alone distinguishes the noble from the base, the
gentle knight from the churl and the savage; which
rates our life far, far beneath the pitch of our honor,
raises us victorious over pain, toil, and suffering, and
teaches us to fear no evil but disgrace. Thou art no 400
Christian, Rebecca; and to thee are unknown those high
feelings which swell the bosom of a noble maiden when
her lover hath done some deed of emprize which sanc-
tions his flame. Chivalry!—why, maiden, she is the
nurse of pure and high affection—the stay of the op- 405
pressed, the redresser of grievances, the curb of the
power of the tyrant. Nobility were but an empty name

[1] A funereal coat-of-arms.

without her, and liberty finds the best protection in her lance and her sword."

"I am, indeed," said Rebecca, "sprung from a race 410 whose courage was distinguished in the defence of their own land, but who warred not, even while yet a nation, save at the command of the Deity, or in defending their country from oppression. The sound of the trumpet wakes Judah no longer, and her despised children are 415 now but the unresisting victims of hostile and military oppression. Well hast thou spoken, sir knight,—until the God of Jacob shall raise up for his chosen people a second Gideon [1] or a new Maccabeus,[2] it ill beseemeth the Jewish damsel to speak of battle or of war." 420

The high-minded maiden concluded the argument in a tone of sorrow, which deeply expressed her sense of the degradation of her people, embittered perhaps by the idea that Ivanhoe considered her as one not entitled to interfere in a case of honor, and incapable of 425 entertaining or expressing sentiments of honor and generosity.

"How little he knows this bosom," she said, "to imagine that cowardice or meanness of soul must needs be its guests, because I have censured the fantastic chivalry 430 of the Nazarenes! Would to Heaven that the shedding of mine own blood, drop by drop, could redeem the captivity of Judah! Nay, would to God it could avail to set free my father, and this his benefactor, from the chains of the oppressor! The proud Christian should then see 435 whether the daughter of God's chosen people dared not to die as bravely as the vainest Nazarene maiden, that

---

[1] See *Judges*, vi.–viii.

[2] Judah Maccabeus, who reconquered Jerusalem, purified the temple, and restored the ancient service (164 B.C.).

boasts her descent from some petty chieftain of the rude
and frozen north !"

She then looked towards the couch of the wounded 440
knight.

" He sleeps," she said ; " nature exhausted by suffer-
ance and the waste of spirits, his wearied frame embraces
the first moment of temporary relaxation to sink into
slumber.   Alas ! is it a crime that I should look upon 445
him, when it may be for the last time ?—when yet but
a short space, and those fair features will be no longer
animated by the bold and buoyant spirit which forsakes
them not even in sleep !—when the nostril shall be dis-
tended, the mouth agape, the eyes fixed and bloodshot ; 450
and when the proud and noble knight may be trodden
on by the lowest caitiff of this accursed castle, yet stir
not when the heel is lifted up against him !—And my
father !—oh, my father ! evil is it with his daughter, when
his gray hairs are not remembered because of the golden 455
locks of youth !—What know I but that these evils are
the messengers of Jehovah's wrath to the unnatural child
who thinks of a stranger's captivity before a parent's ?
who forgets the desolation of Judah, and looks upon the
comeliness of a Gentile and a stranger ?—But I will tear 460
this folly from my heart, though every fibre bleed as I
rend it away !"

She wrapped herself closely in her veil, and sat down
at a distance from the couch of the wounded knight, with
her back turned towards it, fortifying, or endeavoring to 465
fortify her mind, not only against the impending evils
from without, but also against those treacherous feelings
which assailed her from within.

At this moment the besiegers caught sight of the red
flag upon the angle of the tower.   The good yeoman 470

Locksley was the first who was aware of it, as he was hasting to the outwork, impatient to see the progress of the assault.

"Saint George!" he cried, "Merry Saint George for England!—To the charge, bold yeomen!—why leave ye 475 the good knight and noble Cedric to storm the pass alone?—make in,[1] mad priest, show thou canst fight for thy rosary,—make in, brave yeomen!—the castle is ours, we have friends within—See yonder flag, it is the appointed signal—Torquilstone is ours! Think of honor, 480 think of spoil—One effort, and the place is ours!"

With that he bent his good bow, and sent a shaft right through the breast of one of the men-at-arms, who, under De Bracy's direction, was loosening a fragment from one of the battlements to precipitate on the heads of 485 Cedric and the Black Knight. A second soldier caught from the hands of the dying man the iron crow, with which he heaved at and had loosened the stone pinnacle, when, receiving an arrow through his head-piece, he dropped from the battlements into the moat a dead man. 490 The men-at-arms were daunted, for no armor seemed proof against the shot of this tremendous archer.

"Do you give ground, base knaves!" said De Bracy; "*Mount joye, Saint Denis!*[2]—Give me the lever."

And, snatching it up, he again assailed the loosened 495 pinnacle, which was of weight enough, if thrown down, not only to have destroyed the remnant of the drawbridge, which sheltered the two foremost assailants, but also to have sunk the rude float of planks over which

---

[1] Advance; *make* being used as in *make for* a place, *make towards* it, etc.

[2] The patron saint of France, whose name was the national warcry.

they had crossed. All saw the danger, and the boldest, 500
even the stout friar himself, avoided setting foot on the
raft. Thrice did Locksley bend his shaft against De
Bracy, and thrice did his arrow bound back from the
knight's armor of proof. He then began to call out,
" Comrades! friends! noble Cedric! bear back, and let 505
the ruin fall."

His warning voice was unheard, for the din which the
knight himself occasioned by his strokes upon the postern would have drowned twenty war-trumpets. The
faithful Gurth indeed sprung forward on the planked 510
bridge, to warn Cedric of his impending fate, or to share
it with him. But his warning would have come too late;
the massive pinnacle already tottered, and De Bracy,
who still heaved at his task, would have accomplished
it, had not the voice of the Templar sounded close in 515
his ear.

" All is lost, De Bracy, the castle burns."

" Thou art mad to say so!" replied the knight.

" It is all in a light flame on the western side. I have
striven in vain to extinguish it."   520

With the stern coolness which formed the basis of his
character, Brian de Bois - Guilbert communicated this
hideous intelligence, which was not so calmly received
by his astonished comrade.

" Saints of Paradise!" said De Bracy; " what is to be 525
done? I vow to Saint Nicolas of Limoges[1] a candle-
stick of pure gold—"

" Spare thy vow," said the Templar, " and mark me.
Lead thy men down, as if to a sally; throw the postern-
gate open — there are but two men who occupy the 530
float; fling them into the moat and push across for the

---

[1] An old city in France.

barbican. I will charge from the main gate, and attack the barbican on the outside ; and if we can regain that post, be assured we shall defend ourselves until we are relieved, or at least till they grant us fair quar- 535 ter."

De Bracy hastily drew his men together, and rushed down to the postern-gate, which he caused instantly to be thrown open. But scarce was this done ere the portentous strength of the Black Knight forced his 540 way inward in despite of De Bracy and his followers. Two of the foremost instantly fell, and the rest gave way, notwithstanding all their leader's efforts to stop them.

"Dogs !" said De Bracy, "will ye let *two* men win our 545 only pass for safety? The castle burns behind us, villains !—let despair give you courage, or let me forward, I will cope with this champion myself."

And well and chivalrous did De Bracy that day maintain the fame he had acquired in the civil wars of that 550 dreadful period. The vaulted passage to which the postern gave entrance, and in which these two redoubted champions were now fighting hand to hand, rung with the furious blows which they dealt each other, De Bracy with his sword, the Black Knight with his ponderous axe. 555 At length the Norman received a blow which, though its force was partly parried by his shield, for otherwise never more would De Bracy have again moved limb, descended yet with such violence on his crest that he measured his length on the paved floor. 560

"Yield thee, De Bracy," said the Black Champion, stooping over him, and holding against the bars of his helmet the fatal poniard with which the knights despatched their enemies—and which was called the Dag-

ger of Mercy—"yield thee, Maurice de Bracy, rescue or 565
no rescue, or thou art but a dead man."

"I will not yield," replied De Bracy, faintly, "to an
unknown conqueror. Tell me thy name, or work thy
pleasure on me—it shall never be said that Maurice de
Bracy was prisoner to a nameless churl."   570

The Black Knight whispered something into the ear
of the vanquished.

"I yield me to be true prisoner, rescue or no rescue,"
answered the Norman, exchanging his tone of stern and
determined obstinacy for one of deep though sullen sub- 575
mission.

"Go to the barbican," said the victor, in a tone of
authority, "and there wait my farther orders."

"Yet first let me say," said De Bracy, "what it im-
ports thee to know. Wilfred of Ivanhoe is wounded and 580
a prisoner, and will perish in the burning castle without
present help."

"Wilfred of Ivanhoe!" exclaimed the Black Knight,
"prisoner and perish! The life of every man in the
castle shall answer it if a hair of his head be singed. 585
Show me his chamber!"

"Ascend yonder winding-stair," said De Bracy; "it
leads to his apartment. Wilt thou not accept my guid-
ance?" he added, in a submissive voice.

"No. To the barbican, and there wait my orders. I 590
trust thee not, De Bracy."

During this combat and the brief conversation which
ensued, Cedric, at the head of a body of men, among
whom the friar was conspicuous, had pushed across the
bridge as soon as they saw the postern open, and drove 595
back the dispirited and despairing followers of De Bracy,
of whom some asked quarter, some offered vain resist-

ance, and the greater part fled towards the courtyard. De Bracy himself arose from the ground, and cast a sorrowful glance after his conqueror. "He trusts me not," 600 he repeated; "but have I deserved his trust?" He then lifted his sword from the floor, took off his helmet in token of submission, and, going to the barbican, gave up his sword to Locksley, whom he met by the way.

As the fire augmented, symptoms of it became soon 605 apparent in the chamber where Ivanhoe was watched, and tended by the Jewess Rebecca. He had been awakened from his brief slumber by the noise of the battle; and his attendant, who had at his anxious desire again placed herself at the window to watch and 610 report to him the fate of the attack, was for some time prevented from observing either, by the increase of the smouldering and stifling vapor. At length the volumes of smoke which rolled into the apartment, the cries for water which were heard even above the din of the 615 battle, made them sensible of the progress of this new danger.

"The castle burns," said Rebecca; "it burns! What can we do to save ourselves?"

"Fly, Rebecca, and save thine own life," said Ivanhoe, 620 "for no human aid can avail me."

"I will not fly," answered Rebecca; "we will be saved or perish together. And yet, great God!—my father, my father!—what will be his fate?"

At this moment the door of the apartment flew open, 625 and the Templar presented himself—a ghastly figure, for his gilded armor was broken and bloody, and the plume was partly shorn away, partly burned from his casque. "I have found thee," said he to Rebecca; "thou shalt prove I will keep my word to share weal and woe with 630

8

thee. There is but one path to safety; I have cut my
way through fifty dangers to point it to thee—up, and
instantly follow me."

"Alone," answered Rebecca, "I will not follow thee.
If thou wert born of woman—if thou hast but a touch of
human charity in thee—if thy heart be not hard as thy
breastplate—save my aged father—save this wounded
knight!"

"A knight," answered the Templar, with his characteristic calmness, "a knight, Rebecca, must encounter
his fate, whether it meet him in the shape of sword or
flame—and who recks how or where a Jew meets with
his?"

"Savage warrior," said Rebecca, "rather will I perish
in the flames than accept safety from thee!"

"Thou shalt not choose, Rebecca—once didst thou
foil me, but never mortal did so twice."

So saying, he seized on the terrified maiden, who
filled the air with her shrieks, and bore her out of the
room in his arms in spite of her cries, and without re-
garding the menaces and defiance which Ivanhoe thun-
dered against him. "Hound of the Temple—stain to
thine order—set free the damsel! Traitor of Bois-Guilbert, it is Ivanhoe commands thee! Villain, I will have
thy heart's blood!"

"I had not found thee, Wilfred," said the Black
Knight, who at that instant entered the apartment, "but
for thy shouts."

"If thou be'st a true knight," said Wilfred, "think not
of me—pursue yon ravisher—save the Lady Rowena—
look to the noble Cedric!"

"In their turn," answered he of the fetterlock, "but
thine is first."

And seizing upon Ivanhoe, he bore him off with as much ease as the Templar had carried off Rebecca, 665 rushed with him to the postern, and having there delivered his burden to the care of two yeomen, he again entered the castle to assist in the rescue of the other prisoners.

One turret was now in bright flames, which flashed 670 out furiously from window and shot-hole. But in other parts the great thickness of the walls and the vaulted roofs of the apartments resisted the progress of the flames, and there the rage of man still triumphed, as the scarce more dreadful element held mastery elsewhere; 675 for the besiegers pursued the defenders of the castle from chamber to chamber, and satiated in their blood the vengeance which had long animated them against the soldiers of the tyrant Front-de-Bœuf.

THE TRIAL OF REBECCA THE JEWESS.

THE Grand-Master[1] commanded Rebecca to unveil herself. Opening her lips for the first time, she replied patiently, but with dignity, that it was not the wont of the daughters of her people to uncover their faces when alone in an assembly of strangers. The sweet tones of her voice, and the softness of her reply, impressed on the audience a sentiment of pity and sympathy. But Beaumanoir, in whose mind the suppression of each feeling of humanity which could interfere with his imagined duty was a virtue of itself, repeated his commands that his victim should be unveiled. The guards were about to remove her veil accordingly, when she stood up before the Grand-Master and said, "Nay, but for the love of your own daughters— Alas," she said, recollecting herself, "ye have no daughters!—yet for the remembrance of your mothers—for the love of your sisters, and of female decency, let me not be thus handled in your presence; it suits not a maiden to be disrobed by such rude grooms. I will obey you," she added, with an expression of patient sorrow in her voice which had almost melted the heart of Beaumanoir himself; "ye are elders among your people, and at your command I will show the features of an ill-fated maiden."

She withdrew her veil, and looked on them with a countenance in which bashfulness contended with dig-

[1] Of the Order of the Templars.

nity. Her exceeding beauty excited a murmur of surprise, and the younger knights told each other with their
eyes, in silent correspondence, that Brian's best apology
was in the power of her real charms rather than of her
imaginary witchcraft.   30

The circumstances of their evidence would have been,
in modern days, divided into two classes—those which
were immaterial, and those which were actually and
physically impossible. But both were, in those ignorant
and superstitious times, easily credited as proofs of 35
guilt. The first class set forth that Rebecca was heard
to mutter to herself in an unknown tongue—that the
songs she sung by fits were of a strangely sweet sound,
which made the ears of the hearer tingle, and his heart
throb—that she spoke at times to herself, and seemed to 40
look upward for a reply—that her garments were of a
strange and mystic form, unlike those of women of good
repute—that she had rings impressed with cabalistical [1]
devices, and that strange characters were broidered on
her veil.   45

All these circumstances, so natural and so trivial,
were gravely listened to as proofs, or, at least, as afford-
ing strong suspicions, that Rebecca had unlawful correspondence with mystical powers.

Less than one half of this weighty evidence would 50
have been sufficient to convict any old woman, poor and
ugly, even though she had not been a Jewess. United
with that fatal circumstance, the body of proof was too
weighty for Rebecca's youth, though combined with the
most exquisite beauty.   55

The Grand-Master had collected the suffrages, and

---

[1] Pertaining to the *cabala*, or mysterious science of Jewish tradi-
tions.

now in a solemn tone demanded of Rebecca what she
had to say against the sentence of condemnation which
he was about to pronounce.

"To invoke your pity," said the lovely Jewess, with 60
a voice tremulous with emotion, "would, I am aware, be
as useless as I should hold it mean. To state that to
relieve the sick and wounded of another religion cannot
be displeasing to the acknowledged Founder of both our
faiths, were also unavailing; to plead that many things 65
which these men—whom may Heaven pardon!—have
spoken against me are impossible, would avail me but
little, since you believe in their possibility; and still less
would it advantage me to explain that the peculiarities
of my dress, language, and manners are those of my peo- 70
ple—I had wellnigh said of my country, but, alas! we
have no country. Nor will I even vindicate myself at
the expense of my oppressor, who stands there listening
to the fictions and surmises which seem to convert the
tyrant into the victim. God be judge between him and 75
me! but rather would I submit to ten such deaths as
your pleasure may denounce against me than listen to
the suit which that man of Belial[1] has urged upon me—
friendless, defenceless, and his prisoner. But he is of
your own faith, and his lightest affirmance would weigh 80
down the most solemn protestations of the distressed
Jewess. I will not therefore return to himself the charge
brought against me; but to himself—yes, Brian de Bois-
Guilbert, to thyself I appeal, whether these accusations
are not false? as monstrous and calumnious as they are 85
deadly?"

There was a pause; all eyes turned to Brian de Bois-
Guilbert. He was silent.

[1] Wicked man. See 1 *Samuel*, xxv. 25, 2 *Samuel*, xvi. 7, xx. 1, etc.

"Speak," she said, "if thou art a man—if thou art a Christian, speak!—I conjure thee, by the habit which 90 thou dost wear, by the name thou dost inherit—by the knighthood thou dost vaunt—by the honor of thy mother—by the tomb and the bones of thy father—I conjure thee to say, are these things true?"

"Answer her, brother," said the Grand-Master, "if 95 the Enemy [1] with whom thou dost wrestle will give thee power."

In fact, Bois-Guilbert seemed agitated by contending passions which almost convulsed his features, and it was with a constrained voice that at last he replied, looking 100 at Rebecca—"The scroll!—the scroll!"

"Ay," said Beaumanoir, "this is indeed testimony! The victim of her witcheries can only name the fatal scroll, the spell inscribed on which is doubtless the cause of his silence." 105

But Rebecca put another interpretation on the words extorted as it were from Bois-Guilbert, and glancing her eye upon the slip of parchment which she continued to hold in her hand, she read written thereupon in the Arabian character, *Demand a Champion!* [2] The mur- 110 muring commentary which ran through the assembly at the strange reply of Bois-Guilbert gave Rebecca leisure to examine and instantly to destroy the scroll unobserved. When the whisper had ceased, the Grand-Master spoke. 115

"Rebecca, thou canst derive no benefit from the evidence of this unhappy knight, for whom, as we well per-

---

[1] The evil spirit under whose power he is supposed to have been put by Rebecca.

[2] A knight to fight in one's defence, according to the usage of the time explained below.

ceive, the Enemy is yet too powerful. Hast thou aught else to say?"

"There is yet one chance of life left to me," said [120] Rebecca, "even by your own fierce laws. Life has been miserable—miserable, at least, of late—but I will not cast away the gift of God, while he affords me the means of defending it. I deny this charge—I maintain my innocence, and I declare the falsehood of this ac- [125] cusation—I challenge the privilege of trial by combat, and will appear by my champion."

"And who, Rebecca," replied the Grand-Master, "will lay lance in rest[1] for a sorceress? who will be the champion of a Jewess?" [130]

"God will raise me up a champion," said Rebecca— "it cannot be that in merry England—the hospitable, the generous, the free—where so many are ready to peril their lives for honor, there will not be found one to fight for justice. But it is enough that I challenge [135] the trial by combat—there lies my gage."[2]

She took her embroidered glove from her hand, and flung it down before the Grand-Master with an air of mingled simplicity and dignity which excited universal surprise and admiration. [140]

Even Lucas Beaumanoir himself was affected by the mien and appearance of Rebecca. He was not originally a cruel or even a severe man; but with passions by nature cold, and with a high though mistaken sense of duty, his heart had been gradually hardened by the [145] ascetic[3] life which he pursued, the supreme power which he enjoyed, and the supposed necessity of subduing

---

[1] That is, take up arms. See p. 31 above.
[2] Token of challenge.
[3] Hermit, monastic.

infidelity and eradicating heresy which he conceived peculiarly incumbent on him. His features relaxed in their usual severity as he gazed upon the beautiful creat- 150 ure before him, alone, unfriended, and defending herself with so much spirit and courage. He crossed himself twice, as doubting whence arose the unwonted softening of a heart which on such occasions used to resemble in hardness the steel of his sword. At length 155 he spoke.

"Damsel," he said, "if the pity I feel for thee arise from any practice thine evil arts have made on me, great is thy guilt. But I rather judge it the kinder feelings of nature, which grieves that so goodly a form should be a 160 vessel of perdition. Repent, my daughter—confess thy witchcrafts—turn thee from thine evil faith—embrace this holy emblem,[1] and all shall yet be well with thee here and hereafter. In some sisterhood[2] of the strictest order shalt thou have time for prayer and fitting pen- 165 ance, and that repentance not to be repented of. This do and live—what has the law of Moses done for thee that thou shouldest die for it?"

"It was the law of my fathers," said Rebecca; "it was delivered in thunders and in storms upon the moun- 170 tain of Sinai, in cloud and in fire. This, if ye are Christians, ye believe—it is, you say, recalled; but so my teachers have not taught me."

"Let our chaplain," said Beaumanoir, "stand forth, and tell this obstinate infidel—" 175

"Forgive the interruption," said Rebecca, meekly; "I am a maiden, unskilled to dispute for my religion, but I can die for it, if it be God's will. Let me pray your answer to my demand of a champion."

---

[1] The cross.　　　　[2] That is, of nuns.

"Give me her glove," said Beaumanoir. "This is [180] indeed," he continued, as he looked at the flimsy texture and slender fingers, "a slight and frail gage for a purpose so deadly!—Seest thou, Rebecca, as this thin and light glove of thine is to one of our heavy steel gauntlets, so is thy cause to that of the Temple, for it is our Order [185] which thou hast defied."

"Cast my innocence into the scale," answered Rebecca, "and the glove of silk shall outweigh the glove of iron."

"Then thou dost persist in thy refusal to confess thy [190] guilt, and in that bold challenge which thou hast made?"

"I do persist, noble sir," answered Rebecca.

"So be it then, in the name of Heaven," said the Grand-Master; "and may God show the right!"

"It is our charge to thee, brother," he continued, [195] addressing himself to Bois-Guilbert, "that thou do thy battle manfully, nothing doubting that the good cause shall triumph.—And do thou, Rebecca, attend, that we assign thee the third day from the present to find a champion." [200]

"That is but brief space," answered Rebecca, "for a stranger, who is also of another faith, to find one who will do battle, wagering life and honor for her cause, against a knight who is called an approved soldier."

"We may not extend it," answered the Grand- [205] Master; "the field must be foughten[1] in our own presence, and divers weighty causes call us on the fourth day from hence."

"God's will be done!" said Rebecca; "I put my trust in Him to whom an instant is as effectual to [210] save as a whole age."

---

[1] An old participle of the verb *fight*.

"Thou hast spoken well, damsel," said the Grand-Master ; "but well know we who can array himself like an angel of light.[1] It remains but to name a fitting place of combat, and, if it so hap, also of execution.—Where is 215 the Preceptor of this house?"

Albert Malvoisin, still holding Rebecca's glove in his hand, was speaking to Bois-Guilbert very earnestly, but in a low voice.

"How!" said the Grand-Master, "will he not receive 220 the gage?"

"He will — he doth, most reverend father," said Malvoisin, slipping the glove under his own mantle. "And for the place of combat, I hold the fittest to be the lists of Saint George belonging to this Preceptory, 225 and used by us for military exercise."

"It is well," said the Grand-Master.—"Rebecca, in those lists shalt thou produce thy champion ; and if thou failest to do so, or if thy champion shall be discomfited by the judgment of God, thou shalt then die the death 230 of a sorceress, according to doom."

[1] See 2 *Corinthians*, xi. 14.

VIEW OF HOLY SEPULCHRE, JERUSALEM.

NOTES.

ABBREVIATIONS, except a few of the most familiar, have been avoided in the Notes, as in other parts of the book. The references to act, scene, and line in the quotations from Shakespeare are added for the convenience of the teacher or parent, who may sometimes wish to refer to the context, and possibly to make use of it in talking with the young people. The line-numbers are those of the "Globe" edition, which vary from those of my edition only in scenes that are wholly or partly in *prose*.

The numbers appended to names of persons (as in the note on page 14, line 374, for example) are the dates of their birth and death. It must *not* be supposed that I would have these committed to memory as a part of the lesson, though it is well for the pupil to know at *about* what time an eminent man lived or wrote.

The pronunciation of a few foreign words not included in the index is appended here:

Asphaltites, *ăs-făl-lī'-tēz.*
Beaulté, *bō-tā'.*
Beaumanoir, *bō-măn-wahr'*
Bois-Guilbert, *bwah-gil-bair'* (hard **g**).
Brian, *brē-ahng'* (or as in English).
de (*e* as in *her*).
des Amours, *dāz-ah-moor'.*
Front-de-Bœuf, *frŏng-de-bef* (*e* as in *her*).
Grantmesnil, *grahng-mā-nil'.*
Hereward, *her'-ē-ward.*
Hundebert, *hun'-dē-bert.*
le (*e* as in *her*).
Malvoisin, *măl-vwah-zăng'.*
Martival, *măr-tī-văl'.*
Montdidier, *mŏng-dĭd-ĭ-ā'.*
Montjoie Saint Denis, *mŏng-zhwah' săng de-nē'* (first *e* as in *her*).
Rowena, *rō-ē'-na.*
Royne, *rain.*

The French nasal sound, represented above by *ng*, is unknown in English, and can be learned only from a person familiar with French. Certain other sounds are indicated only approximately, as they differ somewhat from the English.

W. J. R.

NOTES.

EARLY LIFE OF SCOTT.

Page 3, line 61.—*Strength.* In this use of *strength* for *stronghold*, we have an example of an "abstract" noun, or the name of a *quality*, put for a "concrete" noun, or the name of something *possessing* that quality. This is a form of that "figure of speech" which writers on rhetoric call *metonymy*—a word which means "change of name" or "exchange of names." Shakespeare uses this same abstract noun in another concrete sense in *King Lear* (i. 1. 41), where the old monarch says :

> " Know that we have divided
> In three our kingdom ; and 'tis our fast intent
> To shake all cares and business from our age,
> Conferring them on younger strengths ;"

that is, on those who are younger and stronger. We also find *strength* used for an army (just as we now use *force* and *forces*—another example of the same figure) ; as in *King John* (ii. 1. 388), where "your united strengths" means your allied armies.

Line 65.—*Wassail - rout.* Drinking - bout. The word *wassail* originally meant the drinking of a health. It is from two old words meaning literally "be hale," or healthy. Thence it came to be applied to a favorite beverage of our Saxon ancestors, made of ale (sometimes wine) spiced and sweetened, with roasted crab-apples floating in it.

Line 66.—*Methought.* It seemed to me. Of course it is equivalent to "I thought ;" but the *thought* in it is not from our present *think*. In old English there was an impersonal verb *thinken*, to seem, as well as the personal verb *thenken*, to think. The former has become obsolete except in this compound *methinks*, in which *me* is the old dative case, equivalent to *to me*. In early writers we find *him thoughte* (it seemed to him), *hem thoughte* (it seemed to them), *hir thoughte* (it seemed to her), etc. *Meseems* and *meseemed* are similar old forms, occasionally used by poets of our day ; as by Mrs. E. B. Browning : "Meseemed I floated into a sudden light."

Line 75.—*Wallace wight.* The gallant Sir William Wallace, a famous Scotch patriot of the latter part of the thirteenth century. He was the most successful leader of his countrymen in the rebellion against English rule. After routing the Earl of Surrey in a great battle on the 11th of September, 1297, and ravaging the northern counties of England, he was elected governor of Scotland ; but the next year King Edward I. brought a great army against him and defeated him at Falkirk on the 22d of July. Little is known of his after-life until 1305, when he was treacherously delivered up to Edward, and executed at London as a traitor, his plea that he had never been a subject of the English king being unjustly disregarded.

Bruce the bold refers to Robert Bruce, the most heroic of the Scottish kings. He was born March 21, 1274, and in 1296 swore allegiance to Edward I.; but soon after he joined the Scottish leaders in their rebellion against English authority. After varied fortunes he was crowned king in 1306, and before 1309 had freed nearly the whole of Scotland from foreign rule. In 1314 he defeated Edward II. at the memorable battle of Bannockburn ; and later he gained other victories over the English on their own soil as well as in Scotland. A truce between the kingdoms followed, but Edward III. renewed hostilities in 1327. The Scots were again victorious, and a treaty of peace, recognizing their national independence, was ratified the next year. Bruce continued to reign until his death in June, 1329. He is the hero of Scott's poem of *The Lord of the Isles.*

Page 4, line 91.—*Sprung of Scotland's gentler blood.* Descended from one of its better families ; that is, the Scotts of Harden, who traced their lineage to Walter Scott of Harden—or " Wat of Harden " (see page 5), as he was generally called—a renowned Border freebooter of the time of Queen Mary. Scott was very proud of his descent from this old marauding baron, and has immortalized him in the 3d canto of *The Lay of The Last Minstrel.*

Line 94.—*Whose doom discording neighbours sought.* To whose judgment or arbitration his neighbors submitted their disputes, instead of going to law. We have *doom* in this sense of judgment in *doomsday.* See also p. 123, line 231.

Page 6, line 149.—*As You Like it.* One of Shakespeare's most delightful comedies. Orlando is the younger brother of Oliver, to whose care he has been committed by their father's will, but who proves disgracefully false to the charge laid upon him. In the opening scene of the play, Orlando reproaches his brother for this neglect of duty, and the "quarrel" is the result.

Line 162.—*Prestonpans.* A small seaport about eight miles east of Edinburgh. Salt-pans were erected here as early as the twelfth century (whence the name), but the manufacture of salt was long ago given up. On the 21st of September, 1745, a famous battle was fought in the vicinity between the Royalist and Jacobite forces, in which the former were utterly routed.

Page 7, line 175.—*The quantity of lakes.* It would be more correct to say "the great number of lakes," or "the many lakes;" *quantity* being properly used with reference to bulk or amount, not with reference to number. The word is derived from a Latin word meaning "how *much?*" and it answers that question, not "how *many?*" We can say "a quantity of beef," but not "a quantity of oxen."

Page 8, line 214.—*I had observed some auditors smile.* With *observe* the "prepositional infinitive" (*to smile*) is commonly used, but the form used by Scott is not incorrect. See Mätzner's *English Grammar*, vol. iii. p. 13.

Page 9, line 239.—*Stout of hand and heart, though somewhat dull of head.* In *hand . . . heart . . . head* we have an example of *alliteration*, or the use of successive words beginning with the same letter or sound. The poet Charles Churchill (1731-1764) illustrates it while referring to it in his "Apt alliteration's artful aid." In Shakespeare's day it was carried to a ridiculous excess, and he burlesques it in the *Midsummer Night's Dream*, i. 2. 33:

> " The raging rocks
> And shivering shocks
> Shall break the locks
> Of prison gates;
> And Phibbus' car
> Shall shine from far,
> And make and mar
> The foolish Fates;"

and more broadly in the same play, v. 1. 147:

> " Whereat, with blade, with bloody blameful blade,
> He bravely broached his boiling bloody breast."

Line 253.—*This was really gathering grapes from thistles.* That is, finding unexpected pleasure in what had been disagreeable. The expression is "figurative," the real meaning being suggested by a " figure," or implied resemblance. It is also an example of a " Scriptural allusion;" for Scott evidently had in mind *Matthew*, vii. 16: "Do men gather grapes of thorns, or figs of thistles?"

Page 10, line 255. — *Gualterus.* The Latin form for Walter. Latin was doubtless used more or less in the intercourse between teacher and pupil, as in English grammar-schools now.

Line 266. *Climbed to the first form.* Worked up into the first class. The different grades or classes in English schools are called

9

forms. In *climbed* the effort Walter had to make in gaining the first form is indirectly compared to that which we make in climbing a steep hill or some other difficult ascent. Such an *indirect* or *implied comparison* is called a *metaphor.* The name is from the Greek, and means a *transferrence.* Here, for example, the familiar idea of *climbing* is transferred to a very different kind of exertion, which it nevertheless illustrates.

Page 11, line 286. — *Galgacus.* A Caledonian chieftain who resisted the Romans in their invasion of his native land, but was defeated by Agricola (84 A.D.). The "speech" referred to is given by the Latin historian Tacitus. Being "spouted" in Latin, it was understood by few in the audience.

Line 298.—*Profane.* That is, not sacred, as we speak of *profane history* in distinction from Biblical history.

Page 12, line 314.—*Ossian.* A Celtic (or Keltic) warrior-poet, said to have lived in the third century. Only a few fragments of his verse have been preserved ; but about the year 1760 James Macpherson, a Scotch schoolmaster, published two long poems, *Fingal* and *Temora*, with some smaller pieces, which he affirmed to be translations of compositions by Ossian that had been preserved by oral tradition in the Highlands of Scotland. They were greatly admired at first, but their authenticity was soon disputed by critics, and a long and bitter controversy was the result. It was finally settled that the poems were not genuine, though they were to some extent imitations or adaptations of Ossianic poetry ; and also that, so far as they were genuine, they ought to be considered as Irish rather than Scotch.

Line 315.—*Spenser.* Edmund Spenser, one of the most eminent poets of the Elizabethan or any other age. He was born in London in the year 1553, and was educated at Cambridge. His *Shepherd's Kalendar* was published in 1579, and six books of his chief work, *The Faërie Queene*, appeared in 1590 and 1591. This poem was never completed. Little is known of Spenser's personal history, but nearly all that we do know is very sad. In 1580 he went to reside in Ireland, as secretary to Lord Grey, the queen's deputy in that country ; and in 1586 his official services were rewarded by the grant of the large estate of Kilcolman, near the city of Cork. In a rebellion which occurred in 1598 his house was sacked and burned, and his youngest child perished in the flames. The poet and his wife barely escaped with their lives, and fled to England. On the 15th of the next January he died in London, perhaps not literally "for lack of bread," as we are told by Ben Jonson, a brother poet who knew him well, but doubtless in poverty and wretchedness.

He was buried at his own request near Chaucer in Westminster Abbey.

Line 320.—*The allegory.* An *allegory* is a narrative with a figurative meaning, which we may or may not recognize in reading it. The *Pilgrim's Progress* of John Bunyan is a familiar and famous example. The pilgrimage described in it typifies the progress of the Christian life. A child may read and enjoy the book without suspecting its hidden meaning. So the *Faërie Queene* of Spenser is an allegory, in which the characters represent virtues and vices; but, as a good critic has said, "the beauties of the poem may be felt though the allegory is disregarded, and perhaps the best advice to give to one reading Spenser for the first time is to let the allegory alone altogether "—just as the young Scott did.

Line 331.—*A Border-raid ballad.* Like many that Scott collected in his *Border Minstrelsy* (see p. 16).

Page 13, line 334.—*Was also a sealed book.* That is, it was *like* a book whose covers are fastened together and sealed, so that it cannot be read. Here we have a *metaphor*, or implied comparison (see on page 10, line 266 above); as in line 350 below: " I waded into the stream ;" where the abundant reading at his command is indirectly compared to a stream into which he is free to wade. But when he goes on to say " *like* a blind man into a ford," the comparison is *direct*, and is called a *simile* (a Latin word meaning *like* or *similar*, which is derived from it). The *simile* is always introduced by *like, as,* or some word expressing likeness or similarity ; while the *metaphor* omits these words and merely *implies* that one thing is like another. If Scott had written, " The philosophy of history was *like* a sealed book to me," it would have been a simile instead of a metaphor.

Line 356.—Bishop Percy's *Reliques of Ancient Poetry.* A collection of old English ballads published by Thomas Percy (1728–1811), Bishop of Dromore, in 1765.

Page 14, line 365.—*Banquet.* Is this a metaphor or a simile ?

Line 374.—*Richardson.* Samuel Richardson (1689–1761), the author of *Pamela, Clarissa Harlowe,* and *Sir Charles Grandison,* novels famous in their day, but seldom read now. Henry Mackenzie (1745–1831) was a Scotch novelist and essayist. His most noted book was *The Man of Feeling.* Henry Fielding (1707–1754), author of *Tom Jones,* etc., and Tobias George Smollett (1721–1771), author of *Roderick Random, Peregrine Pickle,* etc., are reckoned among the greatest English writers of fiction, though their works are not suited to the popular taste of our day.

Line 381.—*Kelso.* This town is on the Tweed, only a few miles

from Sandy - Knowe, where Scott's grandfather lived. It has a
ruined abbey, built in the twelfth century; and just across the river
are the remains of Roxburghe Castle, which was for a time the
chief residence of the kings of Scotland. Being so near to the English border, Kelso suffered much during the wars between the two
countries. James II. of Scotland was killed by the bursting of a
cannon at the siege of Roxburghe Castle in 1460. The abbey at
Kelso had been several times burnt by the English before they reduced it to its present ruinous state in 1545.

Page 15, line 418. — *So narrow a foundation to build upon.*
What figure have we here?

LATER LIFE OF SCOTT.

Page 17, line 53.—*Fortune seemed to pour her whole cornucopia
of wealth,* etc. This is an example of the figure called *personification,* by which lifeless things are represented as living. *Fortune*
here becomes a powerful goddess, as the Greeks and Romans described her, with the *cornucopia,* or horn of plenty, as the symbol of
her good gifts to men. Personification is more frequent in poetry
than in prose, but some forms of the latter furnish many examples
of it.

Page 18, line 60.—*As an exhaustless mine.* What is the figure
here?

Page 19, line 91. — *Gentle as a child.* Is the figure here the
same as in the *mists* of the next line?

Line 103.—*Dryburgh Abbey.* The cut on page 20 gives an idea
of the present appearance of this ruin, which is near the Tweed
and about seven miles from Abbotsford. The abbey was founded
about the year 1150, but was burnt by the soldiers of Edward II. in
their retreat from Scotland in 1322. Having been rebuilt, it was
again destroyed by the English in 1544. Whether it was again rebuilt is doubtful. *St. Mary's Aisle* is a part of the "north transept"
of the abbey church.* Scott's tomb is inside the right-hand arch
seen in the cut.

---

* The church, like most Gothic churches, was built in the form of a Latin cross,
or a cross of which one arm is longer than the others. In such a cruciform (cross-
shaped) church, the long arm is called the *nave,* the short arm at the top (or in a
line with the nave) is the *choir,* and the two transverse arms are the *transepts.*
As the nave and choir were built in a line from west to east (the main front of the
church being at the western end of the nave), the transepts are to the north and
south.

THE CRUSADERS.

Page 21, line 13.—*The Holy Sepulchre.* The Church of the Holy Sepulchre at Jerusalem is generally believed to be on the site of the tomb of Christ, though some learned men have held a different opinion.

Line 18.—*The Grecian or Eastern Empire.* One of the parts into which the Roman Empire was divided a little before the end of the third century.

Page 22, line 30.—*The Saracens.* The Arabian followers of Mahomet and founders of an empire which, fifty years after his death, extended "from the Indus in the east and the Caucasus in the north, to the coasts of the Atlantic in the west."

Line 37. — *Mahomet.* Mohammed, often called Mahomet, the founder of the religion of Islam, was born at Mecca, 570 A.D. In his fortieth year he professed to receive the first of the divine revelations on which his claims as a prophet were founded. Before his death in 632, he had firmly established the faith in which more than 130 millions of people are now believers.

Page 24, line 83.—*Clermont.* There are at least five towns of this name in France. The one here meant is known as *Clermont-Ferrand.* It is in the central part of the country, two hundred and sixty miles south of Paris. Several ecclesiastical councils were held here, the most noteworthy being that of 1095, at which Pope Urban II. was present in person, with many of his cardinals, thirteen archbishops, and two hundred and five bishops.

THE CHRISTIAN KNIGHT AND THE SARACEN.

Page 26, line 2.—*A knight of the Red-cross.* That is, wearing the red cross of St. George, the national emblem of England. The first book of Spenser's *Faërie Queene* is devoted to the "legend of the Knight of the Red-cross," who typifies Holiness in the allegory (see on page 12, line 320, above). The 2d stanza says of him:

> "And on his brest a bloodie Crosse he bore,
> The deare remembrance of his dying Lord,
> For whose sweete sake that glorious badge he wore,
> And dead, as living, ever him ador'd:

> Upon his shield the like was also scor'd,
> For soveraine hope which in his helpe he had."

Line 6.—*Lake Asphaltites.* This is the old Latin name of the sea (*Lacus Asphaltites*), now seldom used.

Page 27, line 35.—*And even the very air was entirely devoid of its ordinary winged inhabitants,* etc. This has often been asserted of the Dead Sea; but, according to good authorities, birds have been seen flying over the lake, and even resting on its surface. Here and there upon its banks are thickets of tamarisk and oleander which are the home of many singing-birds. Except on the east side, however, where there are ravines with fresh-water springs, the shores are destitute of vegetation and indescribably dreary.

Line 53.—*A sufficient weight of armor.* The ancient armor was heavy and cumbrous, but training and experience made the wearing of it easier than we might think possible. Measurements of the many specimens that have been preserved prove that the men who wore it were not of larger frame than the average soldier of to-day.

Page 28, line 75.—*The arms of the owner.* Heraldry, or "the science of armorial bearings," had its rise in the latter part of the twelfth century. Some devices of the kind were put upon the shields used by knights in the third crusade (1189); and early in the next century these coats-of-arms (as they were called from being embroidered on the surcoat, as here) came to be transmitted from father to son. By slow degrees the complicated system of modern heraldry grew up. For an account of this, see any encyclopædia under *Heraldry.* The technical terms of the science (like *couchant* in the next line) are explained in any large dictionary.

Page 29, line 1.—*Crest.* The plume, tuft, or other ornament on the top of the helmet. It came to be an important feature in coats-of-arms.

Line 95.—*The fabulous unicorn.* The creature which is associated with the *lion* in the arms of England. A somewhat similar one-horned animal is described by old Greek and Roman writers as native to India.

Page 30, line 117.—*The renowned Norman line.* Normandy got its name from the *Northmen*—Norwegians or Scandinavians—who, under the leadership of Rolf or Rollo, conquered that part of France in the early part of the tenth century. They were a rude race, but soon adopted the more civilized form of life which they found in their new home, without losing their Northern vigor and prowess. In 1066, under William the Conqueror, they became the rulers of England. Of their doings there we shall learn a good deal in other parts of this book.

Line 119.—*Adventurous swords.* Here we have an example of a very common figure or form of speech—the transferring of an adjective from the noun which it properly describes to another associated or connected with the former. The *swords* are not *adventurous* or daring, but the men who wield them. In the same way we may speak of "coward swords" instead of cowardly soldiers. Gray, in his well-known *Elegy*, says: "The ploughman homeward plods his weary way." Any child can tell to which noun the *weary* really belongs. Compare "a sick-bed" in line 137 below.

Line 143.—*Iron frame.* Here we have a metaphor in an adjective. The strong frame of the knight is indirectly compared to iron.

Page 31, line 166.—*As if borne on the wings of an eagle.* What is the figure here? Compare page 33, line 205: "like a hawk," etc.

Page 32, line 186. *At full career.* At full speed. Compare *The Lay of the Last Minstrel*, iv. 566: "On foaming steed in full career."

Page 35, line 274.—*By the cross of my sword.* As the handle of the sword was formed like a cross (see p. 28, line 63, above), swearing by the sword was very common. In Shakespeare's *Winter's Tale* (ii. 3. 168) Leontes says to Antigonus:

> "Swear by this sword
> Thou wilt perform my bidding;"

and again in the same play (iii. 2. 125), an officer says:

> "You here shall swear upon this sword of justice
> That you, Cleomenes and Dion, have
> Been both at Delphos," etc.

Line 280.—*And now wend we*, etc. And now let us go, etc. *Wend we* is the first person imperative, a form not recognized in most of the elementary grammars.

Page 36, line 310.—*A station.* That is, a halting-place for travellers in their journey across the desert.

Line 320.—*Velvet verdure.* For the figure in the adjective, compare page 30, line 143, above. See another example of it on page 2, line 49, above.

SHERWOOD FOREST IN THE REIGN OF RICHARD THE FIRST.

Page 37, line 2.—*The river Don.* In the southern part of Yorkshire, flowing into the Humber. Sheffield, Doncaster, and Rotherham are all on this river; and the mansions referred to are in the same neighborhood.

Line 8.—*The fabulous Dragon of Wantley.* A monster celebrated in several old ballads (in Percy's *Reliques*, Scott's *Border Minstrelsy*, etc.), which had its haunt in a cave in Wharncliffe Crags, still known as the "Dragon's Den." The creature was finally destroyed by the valiant More of More Hall, an old house yet to be seen on the banks of the Don.

Line 10.—*The Civil Wars of the Roses.* The civil contest which raged in England from 1455 to 1485 between the factions supporting the rival claims of the houses of York and Lancaster to the throne. The badge of the former house was the white rose, of the latter the red rose.

Line 12.—*Outlaws.* Of whom the most famous was Robin Hood, who figures in the narrative beginning on page 84 below.

Line 20.—*Stephen.* Who reigned in England from 1135 to 1154, the first five years being spent in a civil war as bloody as that of the Roses. The old *Saxon Chronicle* says : " In this king's time all was dissension and evil and rapine. . . . Thou mightest go a whole day's journey, and not find a man sitting in a town, nor an acre of land tilled. The poor died of hunger, and those who had been well-to-do begged for bread. . . . This lasted the nineteen years that Stephen was king, and it grew continually worse." Henry II. succeeded Stephen, and reigned until 1189. Though by no means a model sovereign, he was far better than his predecessor.

Page 38, line 35.—*Feudal tyranny.* The rule of the great nobles mentioned in the preceding paragraph. The "feudal system," of which we get a glimpse in the following pages, prevailed throughout Europe from the beginning of the ninth to the latter part of the thirteenth century.

Line 56.—*The battle of Hastings.* The battle fought near Hastings on the southern coast of England, between William Duke of Normandy and Harold the Saxon King of England, in which the latter was defeated and slain, and the Conqueror, as William was thenceforward called, became master of the country. It was fought on the 14th of October, 1066.

Page 39, line 67.—*The laws of the chase.* Severe restrictions upon hunting, the wild game in the country being claimed as the property of the crown. See foot-note on p. 46.

Line 71.—*Add weight, as it were, to the feudal chains.* The insertion of *as it were* makes the expression a simile, instead of the metaphor it would otherwise be. See on page 13, line 334, above.

Line 76.—*In short, French was the language,* etc. The remainder of this paragraph might well be learned by heart—or, better, the substance of it mastered—as a lesson in the history of the English language.

Page 40, line 97.—*The Roman soldiery.* Britain was invaded by the Romans under Julius Cæsar in the year 55 B.C. It was gradually brought under Roman rule, and remained a province of the empire until about 420 A.D., or a short time previous to the Saxon conquest. Traces of the Roman occupation remain in many parts of the country—fortified camps, roads, ruins of houses, baths, altars, weapons, tools, pottery, coins, inscriptions, etc. Many names of places are also Roman; as, for example, all ending in *-caster, -cester,* and *-chester,* which endings are corruptions of the Latin *castra,* a camp.

Line 112.—*Druidical superstition.* Druidism appears to have

STONEHENGE.

been common to all nations of the Celtic race, to which the ancient
Britons belonged. The Druids were not only priests and teachers
of religion, but also magistrates and judges. The oak-tree was especially sacred among them, and many of their rites were performed
in oak-groves. The structures mentioned by Scott are found in
various parts of the British Isles, and have been generally supposed
to be Druidical monuments; but this is by no means certain. One
of the most remarkable collections of the kind is at Stonehenge near
Salisbury in the southern part of England. The cut gives an idea
of it. The isolated stone in the foreground, known as the "Friar's
Heel," is sixteen feet high. The other cut shows a *cromlech* (as one

CROMLECH.

form of these supposed Druidical remains is called) on Ridge Hill,
near Abbotsbury, a small town about ten miles northwest of Port-
land.

Page 42, line 155.—*A Sheffield whittle.* The poet Chaucer,
writing about five hundred years ago, mentions "a Sheffield thwit-
el," or *whittle.*

Page 44, line 191.—*A cap,* etc. From this portion of the domestic fool's costume, the "cap and bells" has become the symbol
of folly. Thus, in Lowell's *Vision of Sir Launfal* we read:

> "At the devil's booth are all things sold,
>   Each ounce of dross costs its ounce of gold;
>   For a cap and bells our lives we pay," etc.

Page 45, line 213.—*Harlequin.* One of the chief characters in the pantomime which is a regular feature of Christmas festivities in England. He wears a tight dress covered with spangles, and his wooden sword is supposed to be a magic one. The *sword of lath* with which the jester is here equipped is a relic of the old "moralities," or moral plays, in which the fool, or *Vice*, as he was called, carried a dagger of lath, with which he used to attack the devil, who also figured in these rude early dramas. We have several allusions to this *Vice* in Shakespeare; as, for instance, in *Twelfth Night*, iv. 2. 134:

> " Like to the old Vice,
>
> . . . .
>
> Who, with dagger of lath,
> In his rage and his wrath,
>   Cries, ah, ha! to the devil," etc.

Page 46, line 247.— *The two-legged wolf.* A jocose metaphor for a robber. *True man*, in old English, was equivalent to *honest man*, and is often found opposed to *thief;* as in Shakespeare, 1 *Henry IV.* ii. 2. 98 : " The thieves have bound the true men ;" *Cymbeline*, ii. 3. 76 : " Which makes the true man kill'd, and saves the thief," etc.

Page 47, line 261.—*An thou beest.* If you are. *Beest* is the old subjunctive form. It was also often used in the indicative ; as in *Hamlet*, iii. 2. 32 : " O, there be players that I have seen play," etc. Sometimes we find *be* and *is* in immediate succession ; as in *Richard III.* iv. 4. 92 :

> " Where *is* thy husband? Where *be* thy brothers?
>   Where *are* thy children?"

When a boy says now " Where be they?" it is a vulgarism; but, like many other vulgarisms (double negatives and the confounding of *who* and *which*, for example), it was once good English.

Thou was formerly used in addressing inferiors, as by a master in speaking to a servant. It was also common between equals, especially if they were on familiar terms ; but to use it in speaking to a stranger who was not an inferior was an insult. Many examples of the distinction might be given ; as in Shakespeare's *Julius Cæsar* (v. 5. 33) where Brutus says :

> " Farewell to *you*,—and *you*,—and *you*, Volumnius ;
>   Farewell to *thee* too, Strato :"

where the persons first addressed are his friends, but Strato is a servant. So in *King Lear* (iv. 6. 32), Edgar, disguised as a peasant, says to the noble Gloster : " Now fare *you* well, good *sir ;*" and Gloster replies : " Now, *fellow*, fare *thee* well." See also on page 86, line 58, below.

Line 266.—*I have consulted my legs,* etc.   Wamba personifies his legs (see on p. 17, line 53) in a merry way.

Line 273.—*Converted into Normans,* etc.   The dialogue that follows is an excellent lesson in language, and has several times been quoted in the larger grammars and works on the history of our English tongue.

Page 48, line 284.—*And drawn, and quartered, and hung up by the heels, like a traitor.*   There is an allusion here to the ancient punishment of a traitor by "hanging, drawing, and quartering;" the victim being disembowelled (*drawn* is still used in this sense in connection with dressing fowls) and cut into pieces after being hung. In the time of George III. this penalty for treason was changed to "drawing the criminal on a hurdle to the place of execution, hanging him, and dividing his body into quarters."   This will explain the seemingly inconsistent explanations of "hanging, drawing, and quartering," given in dictionaries and encyclopædias.

Page 49, line 318.—*This second Eumæus.*   Here we have a "Classical allusion," as it is called.   When Ulysses after his long wanderings returns to his home in the disguise of an aged beggar, he is kindly received by the faithful Eumæus, who afterwards helps him to regain possession of his kingdom.

CEDRIC THE SAXON, AND ROWENA.

Page 51, line 32.—*Chimneys.*   In the time of Richard I. chimneys like our modern ones were just coming into use in England, and their construction was very rude and imperfect.

Line 46.—*Our modern barns.*   That is, English and Scotch barns, the floors of which are often made in the manner described.

Page 53, line 94.—*Blue eyes.*   These, like the yellow hair (line 102), were characteristic of the Saxon race.   As the poet says:

> "from the bleak coast that hears
> The German Ocean roar, deep-blooming, strong,
> And yellow-haired, the blue-eyed Saxon came."

Page 55, line 154.—*Balder.*   In the Northern mythology, Balder, or Baldur, was a son of the god Odin, or Woden, from whom our *Wednesday* (*Woden's-day*) gets its name.   For the story of Balder's death, see Longfellow's poem entitled *Tegnér's Drapa.*

Line 159.—*Evening mass.*   Some critics have found fault with Shakespeare for referring to "evening mass" in *Romeo and Juliet,* iv. 1. 38; but mass is occasionally celebrated in the evening in the

Roman Catholic Church (see our edition of *R. and J.* p. 200). In the present passage *vespers* may be meant.

Page 56, line 189.—*Knights Templars.* A celebrated order of knights, founded at Jerusalem in the early part of the twelfth century, for the protection of the Holy Sepulchre and pilgrims visiting it. Their dress was a white robe (see p. 57, line 228) with a red Maltese cross on the left shoulder. Their war-cry was " Beau séant " (literally "good sitting "), and their banner, called by the same name, was white striped with black.* Their badges were the lamb and cross (the *Agnus Dei*) and a device of two knights on one horse —emblematic of the poverty of the order in its early days (see page 76, line 429, below). After the conquest of Jerusalem by the Saracens, the Templars spread all over Europe and became rich, luxurious, and arrogant. Their degeneracy led to the suppression of the order in France, and later in other countries, their property being transferred to the Knights of St. John.

Page 58, line 253.—*Vows are the knots,* etc. What figure is this ? In the expression that follows we have also a Scriptural allusion. See *Psalms,* cxviii. 27.

Line 256.—*Unloosened.* Just above we have *unloosed.* The variation is Scott's, not the printer's.

Line 260.—*In odor of sanctity.* With the reputation of a saint ; a familiar metaphor. So " in bad odor " means in bad repute.

Page 59, line 284.—*His ward.* Cedric was the guardian of Rowena.

Line 295.—*That of the Eastern sultanas.* The use of *that* is not strictly grammatical ; neither would *those* be just right, as *beauty* is not the abstract noun, but the concrete—meaning a beautiful person, not beauty as a quality. If Scott had written " on the beauty of the Saxon lady," it would be correctly followed by " that of the Eastern sultanas."

Page 60, line 301.—*Sate enshrined.* What is the figure here ?

Line 303.—*Capable to kindle.* Good usage would favor " capable of kindling." This " indefinite use of the infinitive," as it is sometimes called, was more common formerly than it is at present.

Page 61, line 329.—*The dark caverns,* etc. His deep-set eyes are indirectly compared to fires in dark caverns.

Line 342.—*Which are to meet.* The collective noun *train* is followed by a plural relative, referring to the persons that make up the train ; but in such a case *who* would be better than *which.*

---

* A horse marked with black and white was called *beau-séant ;* hence the application of the term to this banner.

TOURNAMENT AT ASHBY-DE-LA-ZOUCHE.

The town of Ashby-de-la-Zouche, as it is called to distinguish it
from the many other places named Ashby, is in Leicestershire, about
twenty miles northwest of Leicester. The ancient castle, now in
ruins, is the scene of some of the most interesting portions of
Scott's *Ivanhoe.* About a mile to the west of the town is a small
plain which Scott is supposed to have had in mind as the place
where this tournament is held. The Lords of Ashby were great
patrons of such passages at arms, and the field of Ashby was one of
the most noted in England.

Page 62, line 19.—*Trumpets.* That is, *trumpeters;* the instrument being put for the person. Compare Shakespeare, 3 *Henry
VI.* v. 1. 16 : "Go, trumpet, to the walls, and sound a parle " (par-
ley). For the figure, see on page 3, line 61, above. *Metonymy* in-
cludes a great variety of cases in which one word is put for another
associated with it or suggesting it ; as the cause for the effect, the
sign for the thing signified, a part for the whole, an individual for a
class or species, etc., or *vice versa.***

Heralds were officers whose business it was to conduct tourna-
ments as well as other celebrations of a formal and ceremonious
character—royal cavalcades, coronations, marriages, etc. *Pursuivants* were attendants on the heralds, to assist them in their duties.

Line 21.—*The quality of the knights.* That is, their rank and
title.

Page 64, line 70.—*The pit of a theatre.* The lower floor of a
theatre, formerly called the *pit,* used to be considered the least de-
sirable part of the house and was given up to the poorer class of
spectators.

Page 66, line 125.—*Burghers.* Inhabitants of a burgh, borough,
or town, of a rank corresponding to that of the *yeomen* in the country. It is equivalent to *burgesses* on p. 69.

Line 129. *Dog of an unbeliever.* The metaphor is contemptuous, like *whelp of a she-wolf* below.

Line 137.—*Gaberdine.* This garment was much worn by Jews.

---

* Most rhetoricians make a distinction between *metonymy* and *synecdoche,* putting all forms of " a part for the whole" under the latter ; but as Prof. A. S. Hill
says in his excellent *Principles of Rhetoric,* "there is no important distinction
between synecdoche and metonymy."

Shylock, in the *Merchant of Venice* (i. 3. 113), speaks of his " Jewish gaberdine."

Page 67, line 170.—*White as pearl.* What is the figure? What would it be if Scott had written " her teeth of pearl ?"

Page 69, line 222.—*Largesse, largesse.* As Scott says, this was the cry with which the heralds acknowledged the gifts made to them ; but they seem also to have used it in expectation of receiving such gifts, or as a hint that the *largess* would be welcome.

Page 72, line 306.—*To break the weapon athwart,* etc. We often find in Shakespeare and other writers of that day figurative references to this clumsiness. For instance, in *Much Ado about Nothing* (v. 1. 139), where Benedick and Claudio are engaged in a contest of wit, the former says : " Sir, I shall meet your wit in the career, an you charge it against me : I pray you choose another subject." Claudio replies sarcastically : " Nay, then, give him another staff ; this last was broke cross."

Line 325.—*Applauses.* Expressions of applause ; a use of the plural somewhat uncommon, though we use *praises, congratulations,* etc., in a similar way.

Page 76, line 445.—*With the shock of a thunderbolt.* That is, as with the shock, etc. What is the figure ?

Page 77, line 452.—*Seemed to flash fire.* The use of *seemed* makes the figure a simile.

Line 472.—*Fair and forcibly.* For the alliteration, see on page 9, line 239, above.

Line 481.—*The bars.* That is, the bars of the front of the helmet.

Page 78, line 489.—*Stung.* Note the figurative use of the word.

Page 82, line 597.—*The Wardour Manuscript.* The source from which the author of *Ivanhoe* professed to have drawn his materials. Of these he says, in the " dedicatory epistle " of the novel : " They may be chiefly found in the singular Anglo-Norman MS. which Sir Arthur Wardour preserves with such jealous care in the third drawer of his oaken cabinet, scarcely allowing any one to touch it, and being himself not able to read one syllable of its contents."

Line 608.—*Gradually and gracefully.* Of what is this an example ?

ARCHERY—ROBIN HOOD.

Page 84, line 24.—*Saint Hubert.* According to the legend, Hubert was a gay French nobleman, who was so fond of the chase that he followed it even on fast-days. While hunting in the Forest of Ardennes during Holy Week, he met with a milk-white stag bearing a crucifix between its horns. Overcome with awe and contrition, he became a hermit in the forest, and preached Christianity to the robbers and outlaws who infested it. Afterwards he studied for the priesthood, and was eventually made bishop of Liége in Belgium. He was buried in the church of St. Peter in that city, but his body was afterwards removed to the abbey church of the Benedictines of Ardennes. He is the patron of the chase and of dogs, and chapels are erected to him in forests for the use of devout huntsmen.

Page 85, line 27.—*The royal forests of Needwood and Charnwood.* The former of these forests is in Staffordshire. In the time of Elizabeth it was twenty-four miles in circumference, but comparatively small portions of it now remain. The most picturesque of these are between Burton-on-Trent and the river Dove. *Charnwood Forest* is between Ashby-de-la-Zouche and Leicester, but is greatly changed from its ancient condition, when "a squirrel might hop six miles from tree to tree without touching the ground, and a traveller might journey from Beaumanoir to Bardon on a summer day without once seeing the sun."

Line 34.—*Newmarket.* This "cradle of horse-racing" is partly in Cambridgeshire and partly in Suffolk. Seven race-meetings occur here during the year, while no other town in England can boast more than two. The population is largely made up of horse-jockeys, trainers, and persons otherwise concerned with "the turf."

Page 86, line 58.—*Your grace.* Observe that Locksley, in addressing the Prince, uses the pronoun *you*, while the Prince uses *thou* in speaking to him. See on page 47, line 261, above.

Line 66.—*Carriest.* Dost carry off, or win.

Page 87, line 88.—*A shot at rovers.* Shooting at such long range that the arrow was not aimed point-blank but with an elevation. Strong and heavy arrows, called *rovers*, were employed in such archery.

Line 108.—*Sith.* The full form of the word was *sithence*, which Shakespeare uses in *Coriolanus*, iii. I. 47: "Have you informed them sithence?"

Page 89, line 156.—*Which it split to shivers.* In the *Lady of the Lake* (v. 621) Douglas performs a similar feat in the archery contest at Stirling :

> " The Douglas drew a bow of might,—
> His first shaft centred in the white,
> And when in turn he shot again,
> His second split the first in twain."

Page 90, line 194.—*I give him the bucklers.* Shakespeare uses the same expression figuratively in *Much Ado* (v. 1. 17), where Benedick says to Margaret : " I give thee the bucklers ;" that is, I give up the contest of wit.

Line 197.—*Shoot at the edge of our parson's whittle.* So Jack Falstaff (in Shakespeare's 2 *Henry IV.* iii. 2. 286) says of the slender Shadow : " give me this man : he presents no mark to the enemy ; the foeman may with as great aim level at the edge of a penknife."

Line 201.—*Cowardly dog!* Compare page 66, line 129, above.

Page 91, line 226.—*Your royal brother.* John was the younger brother of Richard I., who had conferred upon him earldoms amounting to nearly a third of the kingdom. John nevertheless endeavored to seize the crown during Richard's captivity in Austria. His brother pardoned this treachery, and when dying is said to have named John as his successor.

THE SIEGE OF TORQUILSTONE.

Page 93, line 22.—*As well, and better than he could have expected.* The grammatical construction is incomplete. It should read, " as well as, and better than," etc., or, preferably, " as well as he could have expected, and better."

Page 94, line 49.—*Heavy yet hasty.* Besides the alliteration (of which we have noted only a few out of many instances in the preceding pages), we have here an example of *antithesis* (a Greek word meaning a setting against or opposite), the contrast or opposition of words or sentiments. It is a forcible figure if judiciously used. Compare Pope's familiar line, " To err is human, to forgive divine ;" and his translation from Horace, " He 's armed without that 's innocent within," etc. See also line 60 below.

Page 96, line 82.—*The distant muttering of the storm,* etc. Is this literal or figurative language ?

Page 98, line 138.—*Who they be.* See on page 47, line 261, above.

Line 148.—*Azure.* The heraldic term for blue ; as *gules* for red, *vert* for green, *sable* for black, etc.

Line 150.—*It might now be mine own.* Referring in a half-sportive way to his imprisonment.

Page 99, line 175.—*Beau-séant!* See on page 56, line 189, above.

Page 100, line 194.—*Armor of proof.* This use of *proof* was a technical term, implying that the armor had been *proved*, or tested, or would bear the *proof* of actual service in war. The word is sometimes put, by metonymy, for the armor itself, as in Shakespeare's *Richard III.* v. 3. 219 :

> "ten thousand soldiers,
> Armed in proof, and led by shallow Richmond."

Page 101, line 229.—*Blench from the helm*, etc. Shrink from, or desert it. Translate the figurative into literal language ; and also in lines 241–243 below.

Page 102, line 251.—*Holy prophets of the law!* Note that all the exclamations of Rebecca are in keeping with her Jewish nationality. Contrast with these the language of Ivanhoe on the next page, lines 290, 299, etc.

Line 267.—*Like an oak*, etc. Name and explain the figure. In *steel* we have a form of metonymy—the material put for the thing made of it.

Page 103, line 283.—*Thine own image.* A Scriptural allusion. See *Genesis*, i. 26.

Line 288.—*Like crushed reptiles.* Point out another example of the same figure on this page.

Line 305.—*O men, if ye be indeed men*, etc. Observe that this is not actually said to the soldiers outside, who could not hear her voice, even if she dared to make herself known to them at this time. It is an example of the rhetorical figure called *apostrophe* (a Greek word meaning a turning away), which is a turning aside from the direct discourse to address some other person, often not present, or some thing which is personified. Thus Byron, in his poem of *Childe Harold*, introduces the famous apostrophe to the ocean, beginning "Roll on, thou deep and dark blue ocean, roll !" Of course the ocean must be viewed as an intelligent being, or personified, before it can be addressed. In the present passage, the apostrophe is merely an indirect or figurative way of expressing Rebecca's earnest wish that the victors might spare the vanquished. She *would* plead thus with them if it were possible to do so.

Page 104, line 330.—*On a field-sable.* On a black surface ; the language of heraldry. See on page 98, line 148, above.

Page 105, line 366.—*Mêlée.* Confused conflict ; a French word, literally meaning a mixture. It has been Anglicized (or made an English word) as *mellay* or *melley*, which is used in poetry, and occasionally in prose. See, for example, Tennyson's *Princess,* v. 491 : " He rode the mellay, lord of the ringing lists ;" and one of Mr. W. H. Russell's Crimean letters to the London *Times :* " crowded together in one indiscriminate melley."

Note the figures in this passage, and in lines 371, 372 below, where there is also a Scriptural allusion. The next page abounds in examples of figurative language. Observe the personification of Chivalry in 405 and the lines that follow.

Page 108, line 455.—*Gray hairs.* What form of metonymy have we here ? See on page 62, line 19, above.

Page 109, line 494.—*Mount joye, Saint Denis !* More correctly *Montjoye* (or *Montjoie*) *Saint Denis !* This French war-cry dates back at least to the fifth century. We have met with no explanation of its origin.

Page 111, line 549.—*Well and chivalrous.* The adverbial use of *chivalrous* seems to be in imitation of the old confusion of adjective and adverb of which we have many examples in Shakespeare and earlier writers. Compare *fair and true,* page 77, line 480, above.

Page 112, line 573.—*I yield me.* I yield myself. The use of the personal pronoun for the reflexive was once common, but is now admissible only in poetry or, as here, in imitation of the language of the olden time.

Line 596.—*Dispirited and despairing.* Of what is this an example ?

Page 113, line 612.—*Prevented from observing either.* This is the reading of the standard editions of *Ivanhoe,* but there is either some corruption of the text or carelessness in composition. It is not clear to what *either* refers. The most plausible explanation is that it means *either party*—the assailants or the defenders.

Page 114, line 642.—*Recks.* Cares ; now little used except in poetry. *Reckless,* which is derived from it, was in constant use down to the middle of the sixteenth century, but fifty years later it had become so nearly obsolete that Dr. Richard Hooker (1553-1600) thought it necessary to explain its meaning in a marginal note. It was afterwards revived, and is now familiar to every English-speaking person. *Reck* was formerly used impersonally also ; as in Milton's *Comus,* 404 : " Of night or loneliness it recks me not ;" that is, I do not care for them, or regard them.

Line 652.—*Hound of the Temple.* Compare page 66, line 129, and page 90, line 201. Metaphors taken from the names of animals are common, not only in books but in every-day speech. Such use of *hog, bear, fox, goose,* etc., will occur to young people at once, and they can easily make out a long list of similar names. Sometimes the metaphor takes the form of a verb; as in *dog,* to follow like a dog. Compare *Comus,* 405 (the next line to the one quoted in the preceding note) : " I fear the dread events that dog them both."

THE TRIAL OF REBECCA THE JEWESS.

Brian de Bois-Guilbert has carried Rebecca against her will to Templestowe, an establishment of the Templars, contrary to the rule forbidding a woman to be lodged in any of their houses. The fact is discovered by the Grand Master, and the Templar, in order that he may escape the penalty he has incurred, allows the Jewess to be accused of exercising a magic power over him.

Magic and witchcraft were generally believed in, even by the most learned men, at that time and for centuries afterwards. It was not until the latter part of the sixteenth century that any English writer ventured to attack the popular belief. In 1584 Reginald Scot published his *Discoverie of Witchcraft,* in which he exposed the pretensions of the magicians ; but he made many enemies by it. His book was received with much less favor than King James's *Demonology,* brought out a few years later, in which sorcery and witchcraft were treated as sober realities. Executions of persons charged with being witches took place in Europe as late as 1793 (a hundred years after the " Salem witchcraft " here); and no longer ago than 1863 a reputed wizard was drowned in a pond at Hedingham, England, by a mob of his neighbors.

Page 118, line 69.—*Advantage.* Rarely used as a verb now, but formerly common enough. Compare Shakespeare's *Julius Cæsar,* iii. 1. 242 : " It shall advantage more than do us wrong."

Line 80.—*Affirmance.* Affirmation; rarely used except in legal language.

Weigh down. For the figure compare page 40, line 71, and page 122, line 188.

Page 121, line 161.—*Vessel of perdition.* Probably suggested by " vessel of wrath " in *Romans,* ix. 22.

Line 166.—*Repentance not to be repented of.* See 2 *Corinthians,* vii. 10.

Page 122, line 183.—*As this thin and light glove,* etc. Here we have the full and formal statement of the simile. Note how aptly

Rebecca turns the figure against Beaumanoir in her reply, which also illustrates the difference between the simile and the metaphor.

Line 206.—*Foughten.* Shakespeare uses this old participle once, in *Henry V.* iv. 6. 18: "this glorious and well-foughten field." Tennyson imitates him, using the expression "foughten field" no less than three times in his poems.

Line 210.—*Him to whom an instant is as effectual,* etc. Scott seems to have had in mind *Psalm* xc. 4.

Page 123, line 215.—*If it so hap.* That is, happen, come to pass. *Hap,* whether as verb or noun, is now seldom used except in poetry.

Line 231.—*Doom.* Judgment, sentence. See on page 4, line 94, above.

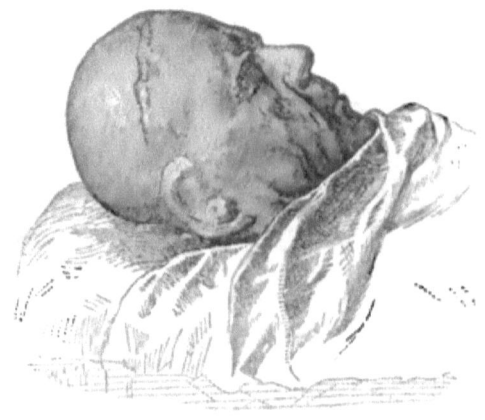

BRONZE CAST OF THE HEAD OF SIR WALTER SCOTT AFTER DEATH, FROM PHOTOGRAPH.

SCOTT'S STUDY.

INDEX OF WORDS AND PHRASES EXPLAINED.

ARMS OF SIR WALTER SCOTT.

www.ingramcontent.com/pod-product-compliance
Lightning Source LLC
Chambersburg PA
CBHW021108020726
47500CB00003B/663